Falling
FOR THE P.I.

a Still Harbor novel

Falling

FOR THE

P.I.

a Still Harbor novel

VICTORIA JAMES

Entangled Publishing, LLC
10940 S Parker Rd
Suite 327
Parker, CO 80134
rights@entangledpublishing.com

Bliss is an imprint of Entangled Publishing, LLC.

Edited by Alethea Spiridon
Cover design by Bree Archer
Cover photography from StefaNikolic/Getty Images

Manufactured in the United States of America

First Edition August 2015

Bliss
an Entangled imprint

To Olivia Miles...thank you for your friendship, your support, and your laughter. I'm so glad we found each other.
Victoria Xo

Chapter One

"I'm sorry, but I can't take a man who wears white jeans seriously," Kate Abbott said, eyeing her sisters with what she hoped was a *drop-it* expression. Really, she hadn't given the topic much thought, but she was running out of excuses. Her sisters gave each other a knowing look and then turned in their seats, looking for another unsuspecting target. Apparently, she had missed the memo that said tonight was all about finding Kate a man.

Kate lifted her pint of beer, taking a sip of the cool beverage, and leaned back in the worn leather booth with a sigh. The Lucky Irish Pub was filled to the brim, round tables and booths packed with friends celebrating the beginning of the weekend. In a town as small as Still Harbor, there was only one decent place to go for drinks, and it had become a landmark in the community. "Besides, it's October. Isn't there a fashion rule about that sort of thing?"

Alexandra McAllister, her youngest and most loud-mouthed sister, leaned forward. "We're so onto you. Finish that beer and find someone who remotely interests you."

Kate gave the room an obligatory glance and then shrugged. "No one here interests me."

"We went to the trouble of getting a babysitter for the girls. We planned this night so you could actually have fun, not act like a ninety-year-old woman with a bad attitude. You need a man to get your mind off everything."

"No," Kate said, making eye contact with their waitress and then waving her over. "I don't need a man. What I *need* is a giant plate of nachos." She smacked her lips together and looked down at the menu.

Cara Hamilton, her other sister, made a sorry attempt to snatch the menu from her hands and glared at her when Kate hugged it close to her chest.

"Hi ladies, ready to order?" the young waitress asked, smiling down at them.

"Yes, I need something really bad to eat, like a dish where everything on the plate is fried," Kate said, ignoring her sisters' loud sounds of displeasure.

The waitress laughed and leaned forward, pointing to some items on the menu. "Oh, I hear ya, honey. There's double-stuffed potato skins and beer-battered onion rings, oh and you know what's so bad it's so good?"

"What, what?" Kate asked, delighted that someone was taking her needs seriously.

"The fully loaded nachos with extra cheese, beef, and guacamole," the waitress said, straightening up and tossing her blond hair over her shoulder.

Kate snapped her fingers. "Done and done. I'll take all of it."

"You got it," she said with a wink and then turned to Cara and Alexandra. "What can I get you ladies?"

"I'm sure we can feed off our sister's trough over there," Alex said, her red lips pulled into a deep frown.

The waitress laughed and gathered the remaining menus.

"Okay, I'll be back as soon as your order's up."

Cara leaned forward. "The point of tonight was for you to have fun, not eat yourself into a food-induced coma."

"You make it sound like I have a complex of some sort," Kate muttered, glancing down at her iPhone display. Relief surged through her—no missed calls, which meant her daughter, Janie, was asleep. Now she could enjoy herself for a little while.

"You do. You need a life," Alex said, tucking a strand of dark hair behind her ear. The problem with the three of them sharing a house was that they knew all about her issues. Kate stared at both of them. They were trying to help. They always tried to help. When they'd first met in a group home, all of them orphans, they had connected instantly. Cara and Alex weren't her biological sisters, but their bond was real and in their hearts they were family.

Cara nodded. "Right. A life for Kate."

Kate rolled her eyes. "Okay, enough. This is starting to sound like a made-for-TV Hallmark movie. I'm a worrier, I always have been. And you'd worry too, if either of your girls were like Janie." Janie was her adopted daughter. The moment Kate had met the little girl, she knew she was destined to be her mother. But raising Janie was proving to be more emotionally challenging than she would have ever predicted.

"Janie is doing fine. It's barely the second month of school for crying out loud. Give her a chance. She will fit in. You know the staff is behind her and our girls are all in the same class together. Cassy told me that Janie had so much fun at recess today," Alex said. Cassandra was her adopted daughter.

"And Beth told me they all sat together at lunchtime," Cara said, reminding Kate of what her daughter, Beth, had said at dinner. "So, no need to keep worrying. Finish off your beer, walk over to that bar, and see if someone sticks."

"I'm not Velcro."

Alex inhaled sharply, gripping the edges of the table until her knuckles turned white. Her eyes were wide and a little crazed looking as she stared at the front door. "Oh, forget it. Our search is over. He's just walked in. *That* is the man," Alex said.

Kate didn't bother turning around. She'd heard that many times before.

"I'm serious. He's walking to the bar. Black hair. Dark jeans. Navy Henley that is clinging to delectable muscle. About as beautiful as a man can get."

"Oh, she's right," Cara said, turning to look at her. "You need to do all of us a favor, so get off your butt and go to the bar. Right now."

Kate frowned at both of them, curiosity getting the better of her, and she slowly turned in the direction of the bar. "Tall, dark, and handsome" didn't cut it. He was leaning against the bar, his eyes on the front door. He was obviously waiting for someone, his dark blue eyes unwavering. He was beautiful in a chiselled, masculine way that made her stomach drop, her pulse race.

"Stop drooling and start walking."

Kate ripped her gaze from the man and turned to focus on her sisters. She had to clear her throat. "I will give you that the man is" —she quickly searched for a word that wouldn't prompt them to force her to approach him.— "fascinating."

"Fascinating? He's not an art exhibit, although he could be," Alex said under her breath.

"I agree. I say we refer to the nameless wonder as Mr. Art Exhibit," Cara said.

Alex nodded in agreement.

Kate shook her head. "I'm not going to refer to him as anything, and I'm not going up to him. What would I say?"

Alex took a sip of her wine and mumbled into her glass. "Try this. Hi, my name's Kate."

"That's stupid. And then what? I'm not going home with a stranger," she said, looking away from Mr. Art Exhibit.

"Oh, I've got it," Cara whispered, clutching her arm. "Ask him to make a donation to our fundraiser. Just say 'would you like to be my date for the Still Harbor Home for Women and Children's gala because I have no life and even less of a love life?'"

Kate yanked her arm free from Cara's grasp. "I am absolutely not asking a stranger to be my date to the most important event ever."

"Then ask him for money. We really need a major sponsor," Alex whispered, looking over her shoulder at him again. "He must have money. Only a man with money can have a walk like that."

"You win. Your conversation has actually driven me to walk up to a stranger in a bar." Kate shot them what she hoped was a scathing look and then downed the rest of her drink. They were right, she had no life. She worked, she took care of her daughter, she slept. That was it and that had been it for years. None of them had had the luxury of doing the normal things young people did. There had never been room to enjoy life's…finer pleasures.

She'd follow their advice, except for the part about asking him to the gala. She'd worry about their lack of funding tomorrow. She looked from Mr. Art Exhibit back to her sisters who were smiling. She took a deep breath and stood. "Okay. I'm going. I can do this. I can approach a random—"

"Mr. Art Exhibit is not random. Trust me," Cara said.

Kate nodded, squared her shoulders, and made her way through the crowded pub. The live band was playing a raucous melody, the crowd on the dance floor cheering. Kate's stomach tightened as she approached the bar. She quickly surveyed her seating options. She couldn't sit *right* beside him. Maybe one bar stool over. Her heart drummed painfully and she cursed herself for being such a wimp. She could stand in front of a room of rowdy teens and she couldn't walk up to a man at a pub? *C'mon, Kate.*

Kate gingerly sat on the round bar stool, careful not to overshoot and wind up on her butt, now that the effects from her second beer were beginning to swirl through her. She stared straight ahead, pretending to be interested in the vast array of bottles on display. The bartender made eye contact with her and walked over. Perfect. Another drink was exactly what she needed.

"What can I get you, sweetheart?"

"I'd love a double whiskey," she said, clutching the edge of the bar and leaning forward.

"Can I buy you that drink?"

Kate stared straight ahead, breath caught in her throat. That wasn't the voice she would have thought Mr. Art Exhibit would have. No, this voice was slurred, rough, and...*slimy*. Because of the loud music, Kate couldn't really decipher which direction the voice was coming from. She turned in her barstool to look at Mr. Art Exhibit. A blond woman was currently draped around the man and he wasn't even looking in Kate's direction.

Kate swivelled in the opposite direction, dread weighing her down as she came face to face with the owner of the voice. He was grinning. No, leering. His long, curly, greasy hair was covering one eye, while the other gave her a slow once-over. Kate swallowed hard. This was why she didn't do bar pick-ups. This is exactly how the Kate Abbott bar pickup would go: hot man ignoring her, drunken man propositioning her.

"No thanks," Kate said, trying not to appear rude while at the same time being clear she wasn't interested. She turned away from him, just in time to miss the visual that went along with the belch that boomed near her ear. *Charming.* So instead of securing Mr. Art Exhibit, she had attracted Mr. Belcher. Kate shuddered, grateful for her whiskey's timely arrival.

The man leaned forward, his rough wool sweater brushing against her arm. Kate bristled, picking up her glass. She downed half the contents in one long swig.

"I love a woman who can drink," the man said, almost knocking her off her stool as he claimed the chair beside her. Kate clutched the edge of the bar counter, while turning to glare at her sisters. Cara's head was face down on the table, shoulders shaking. Alex was motioning wildly, but Kate had no idea what she was trying to communicate. Kate turned back in her chair, ready to take her drink and leave. This was her last pickup attempt *ever*.

"How's about you and I go somewhere we can talk?"

Kate clenched her teeth. "How's about no. Thank you."

His hand made contact with her arm. The heat from what felt like sweaty paws seeped through the fabric of her sweater. Kate stood abruptly and yanked her arm free with one quick motion. "No thank you. And keep your hands to yourself."

"I saw you and your friends watching me, and I know I'm the reason you sat here. You know you picked that seat to be close to me," he said, his face inches from hers, his breath smacking against her skin.

"The lady can sit wherever she damn well wants, buddy."

Kate closed her eyes briefly. The voice. She knew who *that* voice must belong to. It was sensual, deep, and with just enough warmth to make her toes curl. Kate turned around. Sure enough, Mr. Art Exhibit was standing there.

Mr. Belcher leaned forward. "I don't remember asking for your opinion."

"I don't care. Get your beer and leave," he said, standing. Mr. Art Exhibit towered over both of them. He kept himself in peak physical condition, and when she turned again to look at Mr. Belcher, she could tell he was thinking the exact same thing. He scowled at them, took his beer, and left.

"Uh, I guess a thank you is in order," Kate said with an awkward smile.

One corner of his mouth was turned up slightly, and Kate looked up into the deepest, darkest shade of blue eyes she'd ever seen. "Not needed. I consider it a community service," he said, his smile deepening.

"Then maybe I should buy you a drink," Kate said, smiling slightly, finding her ability to flirt. She could do this.

He shook his head. "Thanks, but I'm used to paying my own way."

"Or are you afraid my offer to buy you a drink is really a pickup in disguise?"

This time, his smiled widened, the corners of his eyes crinkled, and his mouth opened to reveal a row of perfect white teeth. "Hell, honey, if that's what you're after, you don't need to buy me a damn thing."

Kate tried to catch her breath, which apparently had been sucked right out of her by his reference to the two of them spending the night together. "Oh, no. That is totally not what I was implying. I'm sorry, this was just me trying to be nice because you saved me from the belcher."

"He belched, too?"

Kate nodded, smiling, relaxing a bit, until three giant platters of potato skins, deep-fried shrimp, French fries, and onion rings appeared in front of her. The waitress beamed down at her. "I'm so happy I spotted you over here. I know you were desperate for these so I thought I'd bring them right out. I've got wet naps and a bib for you, because it gets really messy. Oh, and just wave me over when you want dessert."

Kate gripped the smooth edge of the bar counter as waves of mortification flooded her. She stared at the waitress and didn't dare turn to look at the man beside her. First the belcher, now the food. Kate stared through burning eyes at the platters of fried food. "If you could bring that over to my sisters, since it was meant for all of us to *share,*" she said.

The waitress frowned, clearly confused. "Uh sure. I just thought—"

Kate nodded and forced a bright smile on her face. "Thanks, they were really hungry."

What sounded like a muffled laugh emerged from the man beside her. She snapped her head over to look at him and, she had to give the man credit, he schooled his features to look as though he didn't know she was lying.

He rubbed his hand across his jaw and Kate's eyes followed his hand. It was large, tanned, and the jaw it rubbed against was firm, stubborn. Downright sexy. Alex could definitely pick 'em. "So, since spending the night with me wasn't your intention, how about a dance?"

A flash of heat bolted through her. She glanced over at the small dance floor which had been packed all night. Right now the live music was fast and loud. That was safe. She looked back at Mr. Art Exhibit, taking in the broad shoulders, the wide chest, the clearly defined biceps. No, no, she couldn't dance with a man like this. Flirting was one thing. Dancing...

"It was a dance I was offering. Nothing more," he said, amusement and something that looked like sincerity lighting his eyes.

"Right," Kate said with a nod. "What about your blond friend?"

He shook his head. "Not a friend, just a random woman."

Kate swallowed hard. He was making it clear that he wanted her. She eyed her whiskey. "Excuse me for a second," she said, taking a long drink and squeezing her eyes shut. She shouldn't have agreed to this. This guy just turned down a gorgeous woman who had draped herself on him, and was now here, with her. The only reason Kate was agreeing to this was…because of pride? To prove that she could do this? Or was it him, something about this guy that had propelled her to cross the floor and sit at the bar?

"I'll try not to take that personally," he said.

"Belcher liked that I could down a whiskey," she said into her glass.

He laughed, low and throaty, and Kate found herself smiling along with him. "Well, maybe we should call Belcher back here?"

"Don't you dare," Kate said, placing her empty glass on the counter and meeting his gaze. "But maybe you should reconsider all this. I mean, I still see your friend over there. She's staring at us. I'm sure if you walked up to her and—"

"What if I told you that there's something about you, besides you being unbelievably gorgeous? What if I told you I never dance? Ever. But for some reason, I feel compelled to dance with you." Gone was any trace of laughter, teasing.

Kate took a deep breath and took in the masculine beauty of the first man who truly made her want to forget everything and act like someone who could enjoy the moment, enjoy the affection of a man who commanded the attention of every woman in the room, someone who could revel in another's strength.

"I'm Matt," he said, extending his hand and standing. Kate shook it. It was large, warm, and strong as it gripped hers. The sensation of his hand around hers encompassed everything she'd been trying to avoid—sensuality, desire, heat. When she made the mistake of looking into his eyes, his hand still locked onto hers, she read the same emotion glittering in the striking blue depths of his. She slid her hand free and looked away. It was impossible to feel *that*.

"Kate," she whispered.

"Come on, Kate," he said, tilting his chin in the direction

of the packed dance floor.

Kate opened her mouth and then shut it. What was she doing? She glanced around the bar quickly. "It's just a dance," he said, grasping her hand and giving it a gentle tug. She stood next to him, feeling small next to his towering height, but she didn't have time to react, because he was already walking, leading her though the crowd to a secluded corner, as the music shifted to a slow, sultry ballad, and then she was being drawn into his arms. All breath was stolen as she came into contact with the strong wall of Matt's chest, the clean, masculine scent of his cologne teasing her with an attraction she knew she wouldn't pursue. His large hand wrapped around one of hers, holding it against his chest, the other wrapping around her waist. The band's smooth sound lulled her into a cocoon where this handsome stranger meant something more than a simple Friday-night pickup.

His arms were wrapped around her, and she felt cherished, desired, as they moved in unison. Her head rested against the lower part of his shoulder, and his lips grazed the top of her head, his hand moving up and down her back. They danced like that for a few moments, until his warm hand found the nape of her neck, slowly, gently pulling her head back to look at him. Her mouth opened involuntarily as she looked from his eyes to the perfect curve of his lips.

Motion at the side door as a few uniformed police officers walked into the bar caught her attention. She tried to look normal, she tried to breathe, but between the overwhelming sensations suffocating her and the automatic reaction she had to seeing policemen, she couldn't find a spare breath.

Matt pulled back slightly, looking down at her and then following her gaze. "My friends are here," he murmured, looking into her eyes and then down at her lips. But the moment was slipping for her, reality taking the place of the fairytale as his words registered.

"You're a cop?" she whispered, slipping her hand out of his.

He frowned down at her as they both stood still. "Not anymore. Why are you looking at me like that?"

"I've never been a fan of the uniform," she whispered, backing up a step, hoping the crowd on the dance floor would swallow her. She was panicking and she couldn't help it.

His eyes wandered over her and, despite everything, her body felt a wave of desire in response to the obvious praise in his stare. "Some of the best men and women I know are police officers."

Kate crossed her arms in front of her, chilled. "I wish I could say the same, but I can't. I should really get back to my table," she said, taking another step into the crowded dance floor. "All that food and everything," she said, her voice trailing off.

Matt took a step toward her. "There are two types of people who hate cops. Those who have something to hide and are running from the law, or those who've been hurt by the power of that uniform." He wiped his hand across his mouth roughly, his voice low and harsh. "And I hope to God, sweetheart, that neither of those are your reasons."

Emotion swelled in her heart briefly as his words, his expression, touched her, enough that she contemplated staying, until another man walked in the bar. Every tiny hair on the back of her neck stood. She couldn't see the man's face, just the back of his head. *It couldn't be.* She looked back at Matt who was staring at her, a frown pinching his dark brows together. Panic ensnared her, holding her prisoner. She looked back at the crowd and couldn't find the man again. She stood motionless as her eyes scanned the people, looking for the brown hair, the hunched shoulders...someone bumped into her from behind, jostling her forward. Matt's hands flew to her arms to steady her, but the comfort of his touch was gone.

If Derek Stinson was in this pub, she wasn't safe.

"I've got to go," she whispered, hearing a few loud voices yell out Matt's name. She weaved her way through the crowd, careful to sidestep the rowdy dancers as the loud, fast-tempo music pounded in her ears. Her eyes were on the side door. She needed to get outside. She'd text Cara and Alex. She needed to get away from the man who looked eerily similar to Derek, the monster that had destroyed her world.

Chapter Two

Katie, remember, always, how much I love you and how much Sara loves you. We're always together. Even when we're apart we're together, always. You are my darling, strong girl, and I know you're invincible. Remember that. Invincible.

Kate sat upright in bed, taking in huge gulps of air, like a person who just surfaced from the water, on the verge of drowning, the exact opposite of an *invincible* person. She hadn't had that dream in ages, and she knew exactly why she had the dream two nights in a row—Derek, or the man that had reminded her of Derek.

She threw off the covers and stumbled out of bed, glancing at the red glowing numbers on her alarm clock. 4:38 a.m. She quietly rifled through her drawer and pulled out her running gear, dressing in the dark. There was only one way to deal with the dream and deal with being up this early—a run. After grabbing the bear spray she kept on the top shelf of her closet, she tiptoed down the stairs, stopping for her raincoat and running shoes. Waterproof running gear was essential this time of year.

Minutes later she was well on her way into the core of Still Harbor. She didn't run with music in her ears because today there were certain voices she wanted to cling to. Right after waking, she could recall the precise pitch of her mother's voice, but she knew the inevitable fading would happen, and it would all seem like a distant memory. This morning she wanted to hold on to the sound of her mother, like the little girl who clung to her dress when facing a stranger. This morning, she wanted to feel the warmth of her mother's voice a little bit longer.

She ran harder, faster, the splash of puddles welcome, the heavy rain welcome as the memories grew more vivid and, for the briefest of moments, their sweet voices were louder than the rain, more real than the cold water soaking her feet. She ran, and she didn't know anymore if she was running toward the memories or away from the other memories slowly creeping through.

She was almost at the pier, the memories basically gone. She enjoyed finishing up her run at the pier, with a final loop around the lighthouse, and then a slow cooldown and walk home. It was still dark out, dawn a good half hour away. Her hood kept her warm, the rain dripping off the front, and she could feel the outline of the bear spray in her pocket.

She increased her pace, needing the burn in her lungs to replace the ache in her heart. She was running downhill, almost at the pier, needing to see the dawn, the sunrise over the lake, needing to watch where she was going. *Bam.*

She collided almost head-on with a person and would have fallen into a massive puddle if large hands hadn't gripped her. She couldn't even scream because she was breathing so hard.

"This is what I call fate."

Kate's stomach dropped, then proceeded to flip repeatedly at the sound of that unmistakable voice. It couldn't be. She looked up the hard wall of a chest that was currently sporting a navy hooded jacket and then up into the blue eyes she had fallen asleep thinking about. Matt. She took a deep breath and knew part of her breathing difficulties were due to the man in front of her. "Seriously?" She was about to shrug off his hands, but he'd already dropped them the moment she'd tensed.

He was smiling down at her. "Didn't think I'd see you again. You can't leave a guy standing alone on the dance floor, you know. Bad for the male ego."

She found herself smiling, but then she remembered why she'd left him on the dance floor, so she stopped. "I had to go."

He gave a slow nod, like he knew she was lying. "Want some company to finish your run?"

She shook her head. "I was just about done anyway."

"Ah, you're scared you can't keep up with me," he said, still smiling. He was even better looking than the other night. He hadn't shaved and the hoodie framed his face in a way that highlighted his bone structure. Ugh.

"I can keep up with you, even though you have the advantage of being taller, but I'm sure I could finish you off."

He laughed a deep, throaty laugh. She had never run into him before, and now all of a sudden he was everywhere? She folded her arms under her breasts and narrowed her eyes. He had said he was a cop.

He held up his hands. "I know what you're thinking and I promise this is totally a coincidence. I don't even know your last name."

She made no attempt to give it to him. "Fine, I'll take your word that this is a coincidence. Besides, I'm fully equipped to deal with creeps." She slipped her fingers into her pocket and clutched the bottle.

This time his smile dipped. He even moved back a step

and she was actually disappointed. He recovered quickly from her rebuff and glanced at the bulging pocket.

"Bear spray," she said with a shrug. She forced herself to sound calmer, friendlier.

He gave a nod. "Always good to be prepared."

"Of course, it's a good thing it's not mace or you'd probably have to arrest me or something for having an illegal substance." Hmm, she needed to work on her calmer, friendlier tactic. She wasn't sounding much of either.

His lips twitched and he coughed. "I'm not a cop anymore."

She nodded, pulling her hand out of her pocket. His laugh was entirely too appealing. "So, anyway, I should probably get back home. Morning rush and all that," she said, taking a step back.

He gave her a short nod. The rain had slowed to a misty drizzle. Dawn had broken, but it was barely noticeable with the gray sky and thin fog swirling around them. "See you, Kate."

She backed up a step, into a garbage can. He had the good manners to look down, probably to hide his smile.

She turned around and forced her legs into a jog. She wasn't going to turn around and look at him, because she knew he'd be looking at her, and she knew how good he'd be looking, too. What she should be more concerned about was why the juvenile girl inside her was disappointed he hadn't made any further attempts at getting her number. Well, of course he wouldn't. She hadn't been friendly. She'd been standoffish and bragging about her blinding self-defence spray. She was great at picking up guys. A feeling of emptiness filled her when she rounded the corner onto the main road that would take her home. It couldn't be emptiness because of him, she didn't even know him. No, it was because all the voices and images from her dream had now vanished.

"Come on, funny bunnies, finish up your breakfast, or you'll all be late for school," Kate said to the table of six-year -olds two hours later. Cassy and Beth giggled, spooning the cereal into their mouths faster. Her daughter, Janie, smiled at her, her glasses sliding down the bridge of her nose and almost landing in the bowl of cereal.

"Here, sweetie," Kate said, her heart squeezing when she adjusted the glasses. There were times with her daughter that made her remember moments from her childhood that she worked so hard to forget, images of people who had the power to bring her to her knees if she let them, memories from before she met Cara and Alex. Before she had even entered foster care, back when she had a real family: a mother, a sister, and a stepfather. The memory of her little sister, so similar to when Janie was younger, was achingly sweet. And all the afternoons they would spend together, how she'd call out "Katie!" when Kate would come home from school. Her brown eyes would light up the same way Janie's did whenever they'd play together, or go on the afternoon walks through the woods their mother would take them on, collecting pine cones and leaves in the autumn.

Kate stood up from the breakfast table, her chair scraping against the hardwood. She gave each of them a kiss on the head before walking over to the sink. She was in a good place. They all were. They were all safe.

After her run this morning, and her visit with Matt, she had been able to come to terms with the fact that he was most likely a decent guy. And as for Derek...well, it couldn't have been Derek at the bar. Derek was from another life. They had never run into each other. She hadn't seen that man in almost fifteen years. What were the odds she'd see him in Still Harbor when she was dancing with the most gorgeous, compelling man she'd ever met? Matt should be filed away as another memory. The problem was that Kate could still hear the low timbre of his voice, see the exact shade of his eyes, and smell the scent of his body. It was nuts, crazy, to feel something for a man she barely knew. She didn't feel anything, for any guy. In fact, it had been a policy that had served her well for many years. So why now, why this guy? *Stop the daydreaming and get back to reality.*

"When's the pumpkin parade, Auntie Kate?" Beth asked, eager green eyes staring at her.

Kate smiled, glad for the interruption. See, this was her reality, the one she wanted, filled with family and pumpkins. No guys, no matter how good they looked with early-morning scruff and hoodies. "At the end of the month, honey. The weekend before Halloween."

"And we get to pick our own pumpkins?" Cassandra asked.

Kate nodded, looking at Janie. Janie hung onto their every word and Kate could tell she was trying to keep pace with the conversation. "Yes, we'll all go to the pumpkin patch and you can each pick out whichever pumpkin you want. Then we'll bring them home, carve them up, and enter them in the contest," Kate said, grabbing their lunches from the refrigerator. She lined up the Disney Princess, Hello Kitty, and *Frozen* lunch bags on the stone counter.

"Coooool," Cassandra yelled. "I'm going to make a spooky pumpkin," she said, making a scary face at Beth and Janie who laughed at her antics. Cassy was the most theatrical of the three. Kate had often marvelled at the similarities between Alex and her adopted daughter, Cassandra.

"I'm going to make a crazy one, with giant eyeballs!" Beth, who was Cara's adopted daughter, said, pulling down on the skin around her eyes and almost knocking over her bowl of cereal, which they all thought was absolutely hilarious.

"Okay, girls, let's try and calm down before you spill all your breakfast," Kate said, trying to keep a straight face. "What about you, Janie? What kind of pumpkin are you going to carve?"

Janie's brow furrowed and she looked at Kate. "Happy one," she said, finally, smiling at all of them. Her sisters smiled back at her and then went back to the Pumpkinfest discussion.

She loved how close the girls were, how Cassy and Beth knew Janie was different and treated her as though she was just like them. Kate glanced at the vintage red clock above the doorway and marched out into the hall. It was her job to get the girls to school in the morning and she had this routine down to the wire, no time for fantasies. She dropped each of the lunch bags into the appropriate backpacks and placed them on the rustic, black antique bench at the front door.

"Girls, five minutes and we're outta here, okay?" she called from the foyer. She slipped on her black trench and zipped up her laptop bag.

"I've got three minutes," Cara said, racing down the carpeted staircase.

"Your coffee is in the travel mug on the counter," Kate said to her sister's retreating figure. Cara was never on time. She was a second grade teacher in the neighboring small town.

"Thanks," she called out from the kitchen. Kate gave herself a once-over in the front hall mirror, smiling as she heard Cara greet the girls and offer a round of tickles. Some mornings, Kate still struggled to convince herself that this had all happened. When they all met, in their early teens at the group home, they'd bonded instantly, but they'd each had to move on to different homes and, on her darkest days, Kate had wondered if they'd ever meet again. Well, they had made it, they had found their way together again and accomplished what they dreamed of back when they were girls. They were successful, and they had all adopted their own girls, creating their own family.

"Girls, let's go," Kate called out as Cara bounded out of the kitchen, a croissant in her mouth, coffee mug in one hand and briefcase in the other. She placed her briefcase on the ground and pulled the pastry out of her mouth.

"We need to tell Alex to stop bringing these home from the bakery," Cara said, shrugging into her sweater coat.

"I know. I texted her this morning, after I inhaled one with my coffee," Kate said with a laugh. The girls came out from the kitchen. Kate and Cara quickly helped them into their coats.

"Yeah, especially after Alex and I were the ones who had to scarf down those platters of food when you disappeared on us. Between the bar food and these croissants I'm not going to be able to button my jeans. And then you go off on these secret early morning runs, it's not fair," she whispered.

"Right. Sorry about that," Kate said. She'd already endured the inquisition after she had run out of the pub.

Cara straightened herself up, picking up her bag while the girls discussed whether or not they could bring umbrellas to school. "Uh-huh. Any more news on Mr. Art Exhibit?"

Kate rolled her eyes. "Why on earth would I hear from him? I insulted him, his profession, and his friends. I also never gave him my number, so that's the end of him," she said with a shrug. She hadn't had time to tell her sisters about running into him on the pier. That was not an early-morning-school-rush conversation. She also hadn't mentioned to either of them who she thought had walked into the bar. They would have freaked out if she said she'd seen Derek. She'd been able to use Matt's job as an excuse for her disappearance.

"Well, we'll try again this Friday. Maybe he'll go back there looking for you."

"No thanks, I don't want to keep reappearing there like some desperate woman hoping to catch a glimpse of the guy who has probably forgotten about me already, but you two go ahead."

"If I weren't already late for work, I'd sit here and tell you what a moron you are." Her hand was on the doorknob.

"Go," Kate said, picking up her own bag and settlng it on her shoulder.

"To be continued," Cara said before turning to the girls. "Have a great day, loves! I'll pick you up after school." She gave them all a quick hug.

"Bye," the girls yelled as Cara yanked open the front door and ran down the porch steps.

"We're all ready?" Kate asked them, surveying the three girls to make sure they were properly dressed for the cool fall weather. Everyone nodded. She held open the door, Cassandra and Beth bounding through, and then waited for Janie to make her way. They helped Janie down the wooden front steps and into the car.

Ten minutes later, Kate pulled into the school parking lot.

"Auntie Kate, why don't you ever drop us off at the kissy ride?" Cassandra asked as Kate turned off the engine.

Kate smiled at her in the rearview mirror. "I like walking you girls into the playground and then waving as your teachers come out to get you. At the Kiss 'N Ride, I have to drive away and I can't see you go in." She unbuckled her seat belt and made her way to open the girls' doors. She wasn't about to admit to a six-year-old that she was a total, anal-retentive control freak who needed to see that Janie made it into class okay. She was probably one of the only parents that didn't appreciate being able to use the child drop-off zone outside the school and not having to park and get out of the car.

Minutes later, she followed the three of them to the

playground, marvelling at how well Janie kept up with her more agile, quicker sisters. Kate pulled the edges of her light trench coat closer as the damp, October wind whipped around her. There were still a few minutes until the school bell rang, and a handful of parents were scattered around the playground. Without intending to, Kate picked up on the conversation two women in front of them were having.

"I don't want to sound nasty or anything, but why is that little girl in the class, anyway?"

Kate's stomach turned a few times as she overheard the woman's comment. They had to be talking about Janie. She knew this would happen. Cara and Alex had said she was paranoid for thinking this, but she'd been right. She should walk away and not listen to this conversation, but there was a perverse need to know exactly how people saw her daughter. She justified it by thinking that it would arm her, that she'd know how to deal with whatever they had coming.

"I was thinking the exact same thing," the other woman was saying. "The other day I heard they had to stop the activity they were doing in gym class to accommodate her. And of course I don't want to sound harsh," the other woman said, lowering her voice and huddling closer to her friend, "but there are special schools for people like them."

"I don't see why our kids have to be held back because of one child."

The loud ringing of the school bell drowned their voices out. Tears swam in Kate's eyes and she had to blink rapidly to clear them in order to see the girls. She spotted them, walking toward the doors, their arms linked, Janie in the middle. The girls waved, bright, cheery grins lighting their faces before walking in single file through the doors. The wind had picked up and large raindrops were beginning to tumble from the dreary autumn sky.

Kate glanced over at the two women who were waving

to their children. She should walk up to them and tell them exactly what she thought of them and their selfish, ignorant attitudes. She should tell them how special Janie was. And then she thought of Derek, of his words, his eyes, his anger and, for a second, she could swear she felt the stifling bond of duct tape over her mouth.

Kate stood there while plump raindrops splattered onto the ground and the women walked away, her opportunity leaving, just as it had so many times in the past. How many times had she stood on the sidelines, chewing the inside of her cheek, wringing her hands, trying to find the courage within? How many times had she screamed, only to never hear her voice? She closed her eyes, begging her mind for a release from the images. She opened her eyes again, the playground empty.

• • •

Matt Lane sat in the front seat of his Range Rover, frowning as his best friend and business partner's voice echoed through the speaker. "Sorry, man, nothing. No leads on who this Kate woman is."

Matt let out a low curse. "Fine. We'll drop it. Forget it."

"You still haven't told me why this woman is such a big deal anyway. She was a woman at a bar. Find another one this weekend. I had no idea you were having so much trouble finding a woman."

"I'm not. There was something about her." He let out a rough sigh, remembering exactly who was on the other end of the line. He should end this discussion with Liam before it got extra irritating, but after he'd run into Kate purely by coincidence, he knew he wanted more. He wanted to find her. She was the best thing he'd ever seen at five a.m., and there was something about a woman who looked like she wanted to kick his ass, yet was vulnerable at the same time, that enticed him. "Nothing you'd understand. Never mind. Let's just pretend this conversation never happened."

"Your call, but listen, if you need some pointers on how to do a bar pickup—"

"This conversation is over. You are the last person I'd take advice from."

"Hey, just trying to help you out, buddy."

"Great. Thanks," he said flatly. Liam was about the only person in the world besides his mother and sister he trusted, except when it came to women. The guy knew nothing of value. "Bye, Liam," Matt said and ended the call before his friend could say another thing. He leaned back against the leather headrest and watched the rain trickle down his front windshield. He had no idea why Kate was still on his mind. They'd shared a few brief words, a few moments...before she looked as though he was some kind of psychopath and ran away. Twice.

But he'd thought about her. A lot. He remembered the silky feel of her thick hair as his hands caressed the side of her neck. He remembered the sweet, fragrant scent of her skin and he'd memorized every sweet inch of her body when he'd held her in his arms. The women he met were forgettable, pleasant distractions. Kate had been so much beyond pleasant, and not for one second had he thought of her as a distraction.

He glanced at the clock on his dashboard. Time to get going. The campus was almost deserted as he ran across the parking lot. This was his little sister's last year of high school. Next September she'd be going off to college and he didn't know how the hell he was going to let her go. He'd have to just keep tabs on her. Because of their age difference, at times he felt more like her father than her brother. Knowing she was going off to school soon almost made him wish he'd finished his degree, but he'd had bills to pay, his mother and sister to look after. Regrets weren't something he indulged in too often. He'd made a name for himself, and built a business from the ground up. And now he and Liam owned one of the largest and most reputable private investigation firms in the country.

Matt took the shallow stone steps two at a time and swung open the large door. He looked around, shaking some of the water off his head. He signed in at the office and made his way down the quiet hallway. He stopped outside room 109 where Sabrina had told him to wait for her. He glanced down at his watch—right on time—and then back through the small window in the door.

The half dozen or so rows were empty, as were the seats. A bunch of students were all grouped together around a desk. The bell rang and, after a few seconds, some started filing out, holding papers in their hands. He could make out the back of the head of what was probably their teacher. He scanned the small crowd for his sister. Seconds later, he spotted her and she waved to him. He smiled, leaning against the wall as he waited for her to get her paper back. He was so proud of her. Fourteen years younger than him, she was responsible and hardworking.

Students left, one by one, until it was just his sister and her teacher left. His jaw dropped open and he stood straight as the woman turned, her profile fully visible—perfect nose, fair, smooth skin, full pink lips, long, shiny hair pulled back into a low ponytail. She wore dark skinny jeans that were tucked into a pair of kick-ass boots and a fitted, curve-hugging navy sweater that reaffirmed yet another reason why he'd been so attracted to her.

It was Kate.

Chapter Three

"Matt," his sister called out. He smiled at her, forcing a calm expression onto his face. He looked to Kate, her face going white and then red as he walked forward.

"Ms. Abbott, this is my brother, Matt," Sabrina said, oblivious to the sudden tension that filled the room.

Matt smiled. He tried not to examine why he felt like a child at Christmas, but man, was he happy that he'd found her. "Nice to see you again, Ms. Abbott."

"You're kidding," Kate whispered.

He shook his head, smiling. "No joke. And for the record, I had no idea."

"No idea about what? You *know* each other?" Sabrina asked, wildly looking back and forth between them. Matt cringed at his sister's theatrical display.

He didn't take his eyes off Kate. "We do."

"I sincerely hope this won't negatively affect my grades," his sister said, leaning close to Kate.

Kate smiled. Matt could tell it was a forced smile, a forced attempt at being casual, when she was obviously shaken. "I'll try and not hold it against you," she said, attempting humor as she shuffled papers on her desk.

"Oh, no. Matt, why didn't you tell me," Sabrina said, making another failed attempt at a whisper.

He shrugged. "I had no idea."

"It's fine, Sabrina. Really, I was only teasing. You have nothing to worry about. Your brother and I barely know each other," she said, looking straight at his sister and avoiding eye contact with him.

"Oh, thank goodness. I know Matt has quite the reputation as a ladies' man."

"No, I don't have any reputation," he said. He caught Kate's gaze then, one of her brows arched, her lips pursing slightly. He knew she was thinking about the blond at the bar.

"Sure you don't," Sabrina said, nudging him in the ribs. "Actually, this is perfect timing. Matt, Ms. Abbott was telling us about her fundraiser, the Still Harbor Home for Mothers and Daughters. They need a big sponsor. And it's such a good cause, one I know you'll back. Your company could be—"

Kate touched his sister's arm. "Sabrina, that is so sweet of you, but—"

"What kind of home?" Matt asked.

Kate chewed her bottom lip for a second and his eyes followed. He'd noticed her lips the other night, sitting so close at the bar. Plump, luscious and, right now, distracting him from the conversation. He'd noticed them again when they met on the pier. She sighed softly. "We'll be hosting a gala and the proceeds are going to the cause. We're trying to raise enough money to open a small group home for women and children escaping domestic violence."

His gaze snapped up to hers. He thought of her escape the other night from the pub, the look on her face when he said he'd been a cop. The bear spray. He'd made his career, his entire living, on examining and reading people, and despite the neutral expression on her face, the emotion that shone in her green eyes confirmed this was a cause close to her heart. And she had no idea how close it was to his as well.

"Why don't we set up a time and we can discuss what kind of donation you need," he said, shoving his hands into his pockets.

Kate shook her head. "Thank you so much for the offer, but..." She paused, frowning.

He waited, watching her, wondering what she could possibly come up with to refuse a donation. There was no way she was going to turn him down.

"Don't worry, my brother has loads of money, he can totally help you out with the fundraiser," Sabrina said, slapping him on the back, completely misinterpreting Kate's hesitation. "Even though Matt can come across as arrogant and pig-headed, a bit bossy—"

"Thanks, Sab," he said dryly.

"Wait, wait, I'm getting to the good stuff," his sister said, smiling up at him before turning back to Kate, "but he's got a heart of gold. He's totally covering my university tab and he looks out for me and our mom."

"Okay, I think we've heard enough," Matt said. Kate's green eyes had softened and the corners of her mouth hinted at a smile.

"How about a coffee?" Matt asked.

Kate put down her stack of papers with a small sigh. "Coffee and fundraiser talk?"

He smiled. "Dinner and fundraiser talk?"

She opened her mouth. He pushed ahead before she had time to come up with an excuse. "Tomorrow night, at seven?"

She crossed her arms in front of her. "Okay. Seven."

"Here's his number," his little sister said, shoving a piece of paper at Kate. Matt didn't know whether to thank her or be embarrassed.

"What's your address?" he asked.

"You don't have to pick me up," she said, shaking her head.

"Don't worry about him being sketchy, Ms. Abbott. He's not. He may look a little rough around the edges. He could use a haircut and a shave."

"Can you please stop?" Matt said with a choked laugh, swatting Sabrina's hand away from his hair.

"All right, if Sabrina vouches for you I guess it'll be fine," she said, shooting his sister a smile. She wrote her information down on a piece of notepaper and handed it to him. "Here's my address and number," she said. Her fingers brushed against his, and that same heat, that same spark from the night at the bar, was there. He tucked the paper in his jeans pocket.

"See you tomorrow," she said, taking a step back.

"Looking forward to it," Matt said, ignoring his sister's squeal.

"Bye, Ms. Abbott!" Sabrina yelled, and tugged him along.

"Bye, Sabrina," Kate said, sitting down. Matt glanced back at her before following his sister. What freaking good luck.

"You are buying lunch because I just got you a date with the coolest lady I know," Sabrina said way too loudly.

"I'm buying you lunch because you have no money," Matt said, holding open the door for his sister. He gave Kate a last look, but she was already concentrating on the work on her desk. They walked through the crowded corridor, students goofing off and hollering as lunch period began. Matt glared at a young guy who was checking his sister out and was pleased when the kid looked scared.

"Well, well, well, isn't this an interesting development," Sabrina said as they walked to one of their favorite lunch places close to the school.

"Yeah, a little unexpected."

"You're not getting off that easy. I want full details of how you tried to pick up my teacher." She pointed to the little café with overflowing hanging baskets, round tables, and chairs on the patio. "Let's eat inside. It looks like it's going to start raining again."

"Fine by me," Matt said, holding open the door. He needed to mentally prepare himself for the impending ambush. He couldn't believe he'd found Kate. Sabrina and his mother would say it was fate, but he was more comfortable with luck.

Once settled with menus at a table by a window, he fixated on the lunch items and tried not to make eye contact with his little sister.

"I'm calling the waiter over so we can order and then we can get on with the details of your love life," Sabrina said, turning in her chair and motioning wildly to the waiter. Matt sighed and tossed his menu onto the table as the server walked over to them.

"I'll have the grilled veggie wrap with a Greek salad on the side please. And a Diet Coke." Sabrina handed him her menu. "I bet ten bucks my brother over here will have the club sandwich on rye bread, with fries. And," she paused for second, "an iced tea."

Matt shook his head, grinning. "She's right," he said, handing over his menu.

The second the waiter left, Sabrina leaned forward and grabbed his hand. "Miss Abbott is the best choice you've made since...well, since forever. I want you to know that I fully support you."

Matt stared at his sister. He needed to shut this down fast. He refused to have discussions about his love life with a seventeen-year-old, regardless of how mature she was. "I'm not entering a political race, you know. We're just going out for dinner."

Sabrina sighed dramatically, and he had to hold on to his napkin to make sure it didn't blow away. "It's just that I know the women you usually go out with and I worry."

"I haven't introduced you to anyone," he said, frowning.

She waved her hand. "I may have picked up a tip or two from my summer job at your PI firm. But details, details. Besides, I knew your ex-wife and she was the biggest mistake of your life. The important thing is that Ms. Abbott is awesome. So cool. She doesn't even seem old. Everyone loves her."

Of course Sabrina would mention his ex. He didn't want to think about her. He'd rather think about Kate, the woman from the bar and the woman jogging by herself at five in the morning on the pier. Matt broke his sister's intense gaze and stared out the window for a few moments.

"Hello? Are you listening?"

Matt looked over at his sister. "I'm glad you like her, but I don't think there's anything more to discuss," Matt said, relieved when the waiter arrived, placing their food and drinks in front of them. He wasn't about to engage in any more conversation about Kate, or his ex-wife, especially not with his kid sister.

Sabrina stabbed her salad at least a dozen times before looking up at him. "Lots to discuss, like where did you meet her? What happened? Why didn't you get her number earlier? How come you didn't know she was a teacher?"

Matt swallowed hard. He wasn't going to tell her he'd tried to pick up her teacher at a bar. He didn't say anything. He was always telling Sabrina never to fall for a guy's pickup lines.

"Oh, is this the part in the conversation where you shut down and refuse to talk about your personal life?"

He purposely took a large bite of his sandwich and then pointed to his full mouth. His sister's pretty face lit up like it usually did right before she yelled at him. He sat back in his chair, chewing slowly, and stretched out his legs.

She stole a handful of his fries. He thought it wasn't the best time to mention that she should order her own damn fries since every time they went out together she ordered a salad and then ended up eating all his fries.

"I think she's the perfect woman for you."

He sat up straight. "Whoa, back it up. I'm not looking for the perfect woman. I'm just looking for someone..." He let his voice trail off. He wasn't about to say exactly what he was thinking about when it came to Kate. There were certain topics of conversation he didn't want to share with his little sister. The fact that he thought her teacher was hot and that he was mostly interested in the amazing chemistry they had was not something he'd admit out loud. So he took another monster bite of the sandwich while his sister glared at him.

"Listen," she whispered, leaning forward, blue eyes narrowed into tiny little slits. He stopped chewing. "If you think you can have a quick fling with my social studies teacher then you are sorely mistaken. It's time you grew up and out of your shallow existence."

He placed the remainder of his sandwich on the plate with a sigh. "I get that you're trying to help, Sab, but I don't want commitment. I don't want marriage or kids. Not for me. You can do that, after I run a full background check on the guy, and then mom can have grandchildren. I'm going to be the kid who could never settle down. Besides, you can't tell me to grow up. You're too young for that."

His sister grabbed more fries from his plate, glaring at him. He shoved the plate in her direction.

"I know Michelle did a number on you. I know you have a hard time trusting people. I get it, she cheated on you and now you think you can't trust anyone ever again," she said, waving a fry in front of his face, her nose scrunching up. He looked away when tears filled her eyes. This was why he didn't discuss women and dating with his kid sister. She was a softy and an endearing sap. "But you need to move on," Sabrina said, patting his hand.

Matt pulled his hand from hers. "I have. Michelle is in the past. Just because I don't want to get married again doesn't mean I haven't moved on. I know for a fact that marriage, kids, the white picket fence, and all that crap isn't for me. I don't want it. I love my work, my business. I don't want anything else." He picked up his drink, wishing it was hard liquor.

His sister gave a little *humph* and then took a few more of his fries. He shoved the bottle of ketchup her way. "Thanks," she mumbled, pouring some on the side of her plate.

"How do you know you don't want kids?"

He ran his hands down his face with a groan. "I don't know. They...I don't have anything in common with them."

She put down the fries and looked up at him. "Really? I think you have a lot in common with children."

"You're funny," he said, grabbing one of the stolen fries from her plate. It wasn't kids personally, because he didn't know any kids. And heck, he'd done his own part in raising Sabrina. He knew how much emotional and physical support kids needed. He also knew what a crazy, screwed-up world it was, and having to worry about his own child would add way too much stress to his life. He'd seen horror and he'd witnessed things he wished he could erase from his memory, things he'd never dare share with his little sister, but they were all things that kept him from truly contemplating kids. Right now, things were uncomplicated. Perfect.

"So what do you know about this fundraiser of hers?"

"Not that much, just that she and her sisters are working

on this project. It's a great cause, don't you think? I should have thought of you right away when she first mentioned it last week. I mean with our history, with mom…" she said, her voice trailing off as she swirled a fry around the ketchup.

Matt glanced at the streaks of rain on the window. Yeah, it was a good cause, and yes, it was close to home, to his heart.

The low vibration of his phone against the tabletop pulled him from his thoughts. He glanced down at the screen. "I've got to answer this call, Sab," he said, rising. "You finish lunch and I'll be outside." He slapped a few bills on the table before walking out the door.

"Matt Lane," he said into the receiver, even though he already knew whose voice would greet him on the other end of the line. Finding good people to fill positions in his growing company was difficult. He'd been waiting for this call. He'd asked a retired police officer to join his PI business. Derek Stinson had been his mentor, one of the best men he'd ever met. Today was shaping up to be a pretty damn good day.

· · ·

Matt pressed the worn doorbell and took a step back from the door, staring at the cutouts of black cats and pumpkins on the front door. *Kind of odd for an adult to be taping handmade decorations to their door.* Maybe Kate was into Halloween. Seconds later screeches and laughter erupted from inside the home. He frowned at the sound, internal alarm bells going off. He rolled his shoulders. Just because he heard high-pitched feminine laughter didn't mean it was kids. Or maybe she had guests over. Guests with kids.

He turned to look out from the covered porch. Two large pots of mums flanked the top of the porch steps. The street was quaint and charming, a mix of two-story homes and bungalows. The yards were oversized, impeccably kept, and the sidewalks were lined with old-growth maple trees. It was picturesque, appealing, and idyllic if you were into the family type of thing. Still Harbor was one of those towns that had remained immune to massive growth and change. One of those towns you didn't associate with modern-day America anymore. It had been the perfect place for his mother, Sabrina, and him to relocate to after they left the city.

The door swung open and three curious faces greeted him. *Not* friend's kids. Three little girls, dressed in orange pyjamas that said *"Boo!"* were standing there, staring at him as though he were the most interesting person they'd ever seen.

The tallest one yelled out, "There's a man here!"

Matt blinked. The girls were still there. He had no idea Kate had a kid. Or three kids. Dread formed in the pit of his stomach. Kids made everything complicated. He stared at the little girl wearing the glasses for a moment longer, but tried to plaster a smile on his face for all of them.

Kate's blond friend who'd been at the bar the other night appeared from a doorway at the end of the hall. Relief oozed through him. Thank God. Maybe they were the sister's kids. She approached quickly, wiping her hands on a dishtowel.

"Girls, you know you're not supposed to answer the door by yourselves," she said. She flashed him a smile and then opened the screen door.

"Hi, come on in. I'm Cara, Kate's sister," she said, extending her hand as he stood in the doorway. The little girls still stood, clustered around him and peering up in a way that reminded him of Sabrina when she'd been little. Funny how he'd lost his ability to relate to kids. Now he saw them as complications in a relationship. This was why he adhered to a strict no-single-mom policy.

"Sorry, it gets really loud in here at bedtime and no one heard the knock," she said. She was pretty. Looked nothing like Kate, but she was attractive.

"No problem," he said, stuffing his hands into his pockets. He never really knew what to do around kids. When his sister had been small, he'd quickly taken on the role of the protector, and moments of laughter and silliness hadn't been very frequent.

"Kate," Cara called from the bottom of the stairs. She turned around to look at him, smiling. "She's usually on time for everything, but she's having a few wardrobe issues tonight," she said with a little wink.

Matt smiled. That piece of information was a nice little indication that Kate was interested in more than just a fundraiser donation. Matt glanced around the entryway, taking in the school bags, books, and rain gear. It was looking less and less like these were all her sister's kids. Cheerful yellow walls and homey rugs in the hall made the place feel like a family home. There were pictures lining the staircase wall—black and white pictures of the girls, Kate, and her sisters. Matt swallowed past the lump in his throat. He was already feeling stifled.

Seconds later, Kate made her way down the stairs, and he forgot most of his claustrophobic thoughts. She'd made a pretty good wardrobe decision. Then again, he was pretty damn sure that Kate could make anything look good. The dark fitted jeans and an ivory, probably cashmere, scoop neck sweater looked delicious, hugging every curve. Her dark hair was shiny and loose and, from where he stood, she wasn't wearing a lot of makeup. Her lips looked faintly shiny, very inviting.

"Hi," she said, smiling slightly as she made her way down the staircase.

He smiled at her, liking the way her green eyes sparkled. "Hi."

"You've met everyone?" she asked, slipping into the same

pair of boots she'd been wearing at school. They were the kick-ass looking boots that he found insanely hot, especially on a woman like Kate. He tore his gaze away and tried to concentrate on the conversation that was playing out.

"We met him! Is this Mr. Art Zibbits?" the little blonde girl asked.

Matt frowned. She was expecting someone else? Kate's eyes grew wide and her sister covered her face with the tea towel, shoulders shaking.

"No, this is *Matt*," Kate said in a high-pitched voice.

The little girl frowned. "Oh. So when's Art coming?"

"He's not coming," Cara said, shooting him a wan smile. He had to wonder about this Art guy. Kate didn't seem the type to book two men on the same night, or date two guys at the same time. But then again, maybe she really wasn't viewing tonight as a date at all.

"What about Mr. Zibbits?" the brown-haired girl asked. The little girl with glasses was frowning, looking back and forth between the others.

"There is no Mr. *Zibbits*," Kate squeaked. Matt had no idea what was going on.

Kate glanced at him quickly, before giving each of the girls a hug. He was intrigued when she stopped a little longer, crouching down to speak with the girl wearing glasses. "Mommy will be home in a little while, okay? Go to bed nicely for Auntie Cara."

Matt schooled his features. It was confirmed: Kate was a mom. To one, or possibly all of them. The little girl's lower lip shook and she wrapped her small arms around Kate's neck. He could see Kate squeezing her tightly. Seconds later, Kate stood. "Okay, see you later. Have a good night."

"Bye girls, nice to meet you. Bye Cara," he said, holding the door open for Kate.

They stepped out onto the porch and Matt was very

aware of the eyes focused on them as they walked down the steps. "I feel like I'm in a fish bowl," he murmured.

Kate smiled and turned to wave. "Yeah, I'm actually thinking we need to hurry up and get out of here before they come tearing after us."

Matt's mind was spinning. What the hell had he gotten himself into? Kate was a mother. Well, one date wasn't going to hurt him. He could sign up for the donation and then never see her again. He paused before getting into the SUV and pretended to glance down at his phone. He hadn't made any commitments. It was a working date, nothing more.

He opened the door for her and he could read the surprise on her face when he did. "Uh, thanks," she said, but then paused, not stepping into his SUV. Instead, she turned to look at him, crossing her arms in front of her.

"I just want to be clear," she began softly. "I'm not looking for anything other than a donation. I can tell you're surprised that I have a daughter." Her head was tilted back so that she could look at him squarely in the eye.

He cleared his throat. "So only one is yours?"

Kate surprised him by smiling, and he found himself smiling in return, then looking at her mouth. She was not what he'd expected, and his attraction to her was only increasing instead of diminishing. That should have sent off some warning bells.

"Yes. The little girl with glasses, Janie, is my daughter. She has Down's syndrome. I adopted her. There is no father, no husband, no anyone," she said softly, but in a voice that was filled with conviction, slightly defensive.

He stared at her, speechless, impressed. She made him think of all the good women in his life, the ones who had sacrificed and loved him. She made him think all the naïve thoughts he'd once had about people when he was little, before he learned how horrible they could really be. Her expression reminded him of himself when he'd defiantly look up to his father, hoping for acceptance, but bracing himself for the worst.

He swallowed, hard. "Why didn't you introduce me to your daughter?"

Her eyes narrowed. "I read the expression on your face. I saw the shock and I have no intention of introducing my daughter to someone who won't be around tomorrow. Don't worry, I've gotten used to it. I also know that I've had to choose my...friends wisely. I don't put up with crap from people, so if you want to donate, it will be *greatly* appreciated. If you were after something else and now want out, that's fine too. Just don't waste my time and don't bother acting all charming if you're after a quick screw. I don't work that way," she said, backing up abruptly.

Matt grabbed her hand, finding his voice. "Don't do that, don't assume I'm like everyone else." He didn't know what the hell he was doing, or what he was promising, but he didn't want to be that guy she was describing, and he didn't want to say good-bye to Kate.

Chapter Four

Awkward. Totally, completely, awkward.

She'd just insulted the man who was about to donate cash to a cause he didn't know anything about. Maybe she had judged him prematurely. She didn't like the idea that she was being judgmental, but she was still reeling from the expression of shock on his face when he realized she had a daughter. And yes, she was jumping to conclusions that he had reacted that way because of Janie. She had learned the hard way to assume the worst and it was easier like that, rather than getting hurt later on. How many times had people asked her why? Why would she adopt a little girl "like that"? Why would she do that to herself? So, yes, she'd assumed the worst about him, but now he was sitting beside her, not looking like he was trying to get out of their date or looking uncomfortable. When he'd grabbed her arm, there had been something in his eyes that told her he was for real.

So maybe his reaction was because he didn't know she had a child. *Any* child. She couldn't hate him for that. Besides, it's not like this was going anywhere. Guys who looked like him were perpetual bachelors. Walking into bars, picking up women, going home with them. And really, hadn't she led him to believe the same thing about her? She met him at a bar, and then fled like some manic Cinderella, and now she expected him to be all, *oh I love kids*? Of course not.

"Why do I get the feeling you're plotting my murder?"

Kate whipped her head around to look at him. His eyes were still on the road, but that mouth of his had turned up into an alluring half smile. He was teasing her.

"I'm not. I promise. Well, I'm not anymore."

He laughed, and the sound was so good that she had to curl her toes. It was low, deep, and so masculine. She obviously needed to date more. "You're all wrong about me. While I did enjoy the 'you're not getting into my pants' threat, I'm now going to have to go to great lengths to prove you wrong."

She crossed her arms and looked out the window as he drove them through the scenic streets of Still Harbor. "So that means an evening that's strictly professional."

"I can't lie. If that were all I was interested in, I'd have handed you a check. You have to admit, you're kind of interested in me."

She tried not to laugh. He had the charming routine down pat.

"And for the record, the look you saw on my face was shock, that's it. The kid thing took me by surprise."

He didn't say anything about Janie, and yeah, many people wouldn't directly say something, but then again many people did and had to her face. He was honest and that appealed to her on many levels. "What did I strike you as?"

Again, that hint of a smile played across his face. "A smart, gorgeous woman who was single and looking for...a night out."

"Safe answer."

"I'm not a stupid man."

She laughed. He slowed the car and then parallel parked in one of the few vacant spots on Main Street.

"Have you eaten here before?" Matt took the keys out of the ignition and turned to her. They were parked outside of Pasquale's Italian Bistro, one of the nicest, most popular restaurants in town. The restaurant was a local favorite, offering authentic, homemade Italian food and one of the best views of the escarpment from the floor-to-ceiling windows. A date restaurant. She glanced over at him, unable to deny she was sitting next to the most attractive man she'd ever met. When he'd grabbed her hand outside the car after her speech, she'd felt the effects of his touch sweep through her entire body. She'd been attracted to him at the bar, at the pier, and in her classroom, but tonight, he'd filled their small entryway with this aura of masculinity and strength. He was wearing dark jeans, slightly faded in the front, that outlined the long, lean lines of his body. His navy, V-neck sweater and white button-down shirt underneath made him look as though he took some effort to dress up. And the outfit showed off his wide shoulders and hugged his flat stomach. Mr. Art Zibbits was undeniably hot.

"I have, it's delicious," she said, trying not to look at his mouth when she said "delicious," but of course, that was exactly where she looked because he had a delicious mouth. And smile. One that made you want to keep making him smile, because his eyes smiled too.

"Perfect," he said, and then he was out of the car. Before she could gather up her files and purse, he had already opened her door. He held it open while she snatched up her things and hopped out of his SUV. Minutes later they were standing in the tiny, crowded entryway of Pasquale's, Matt's body brushing against her back. He gave the frazzled, young hostess his name and they waited along with the other patrons. "Popular place," Matt said close to her ear.

A shiver ran through her and she turned around to look at him. He was standing close. Out of necessity, since the place was packed. She nodded. "Best homemade gnocchi in the area." She turned her head slightly as a familiar voice caught her attention. It was that mom from the girls' school, the one who'd made those mean remarks. She didn't want to see this woman tonight. She wasn't even aware that she had taken a step back, until she bumped into the hard wall that was Matt. His large hands were on her shoulders, strong, gently steadying her.

"You okay?" he whispered in her ear.

Now Kate had two problems: the woman and her own reactions to the man standing behind her. She nodded, trying to look calm. "Of course," she said, turning around. He dropped his hands and she looked up at him. "Thanks, I'm fine."

"Oh, good. I was worried you were going to step on me with your kick-ass boots."

She smiled. "They *are* kick-ass boots, how did you know?"

"I know things about people. You're the kick-ass type of woman, I can feel it. So what's bothering you?"

She opened her mouth, ready to come up with a lie, because the truth sounded so pathetic and, really, what was her problem? A mom had made some remarks that weren't too surprising; the sort of remarks Kate had already braced herself for when Janie had started her new school. What could she possible say to this gorgeous guy who obviously knew nothing about kids that wouldn't make her look weak? He even thought she was kick-ass. She was more than capable of having dinner in the same restaurant as the woman who had basically said her daughter didn't belong. Matt was looking down at her with genuine concern in those blue eyes. "Nothing, I uh…"

"Saw someone you couldn't stand?"

Her eyebrows snapped together. "How did you know that?"

"I know things," he said with a hint of a smile on his gorgeous mouth. He took her hand and leaned down, maybe an inch from her body and whispered in her ear. "How about we go somewhere else? No stupid people."

She would have said no, but she laughed at his "stupid people" remark and seconds later they were out the door and back in his Range Rover and on their way. He didn't even ask her about who she was avoiding or why she was so agreeable to leaving. She studied the chiseled, strong features of his profile. His tanned hand hugged the gearshift, and his sleeves were rolled up slightly, showing a tanned forearm and a thick silver watch.

"So, where are we going?"

"We are going to a place with the best view of the escarpment and the city at nighttime. Oh, and one stop along the way."

Her stomach twirled around until it had tied itself into a big knot. This was so unlike her. She had barely wanted to go out with him, hadn't wanted to drive together to the restaurant, and now she was going to some mysterious place. Just as she was about to ask him for details, he shot her a look.

"Don't worry. This isn't me turning into some crazy-ass. It's me thinking on the spot and not wanting to screw up our night. I had wanted to take you to a nice place, and then when I saw the look on your face when you saw the blonde woman, I wanted to get you out of there. So now, I want to put a smile back on your face, because you've got the most gorgeous smile I've ever seen in my life."

Her mouth was open, but words weren't coming out, maybe because she wasn't processing with words, just the emotion that held her firm in her seat. The warmth in his deep voice seemed to envelope her in this cocoon of safety, which she had never felt. The closest she'd ever felt to safe was when she, Alex, and Cara had moved in together in Still Harbor. Safety wasn't a feeling that came easily. So what just happened? She was going to have to watch herself. Her reaction to him was completely irrational. She didn't know if he expected her to say something back, but he was already pulling onto some downtown street of a little village. She recognized it as one of the neighboring towns on the way to the city.

"Be right back," he said, and jumped out of the car.

She watched as he jogged across the street and into an unassuming little place. The sign over the door said QUEBEC BISTRO. In five minutes, he was back out, holding a large paper bag. He placed it in the backseat and then hopped back into the car. "Not that long until we get to my place."

A delicious aroma filled the car and she tried to figure out what he'd bought.

"I hope you like some real, authentic poutine."

As if on cue, her stomach growled loudly. *Please don't let that actually be loud enough to be heard.* The slow, sexy grin that appeared on his face answered her question. "Yeah, I like poutine," she said. "Nothing like French fries smothered in gravy and cheese curds."

"This is unlike any other poutine you've tried, guaranteed. My sister got me hooked on this place. She has a French fry obsession and they make their own gravy. The cheese is from a local farm. Basically, this will ruin you for all other poutines. Now, I just need to get us home fast so it doesn't get soggy."

"Do you live far from here?"

He shook his head. "I live halfway between the city and Still Harbor." Since there was nothing other than villages between the city and Still Harbor, that meant he lived in the country. They turned down a deserted road, with a smattering of pumpkin patches along the way. Matt took the gentle turns with an ease that suggested he was familiar with this route. Seconds later they were pulling into a long, winding drive and at the end was a modern, one-story ranch style home. But it wasn't the home that took her breath; it was the escarpment beyond.

"This is beautiful," she said, unbuckling her belt.

"Thanks. Had it built a few years ago. C'mon," he said, eyes twinkling. "I can't stand cold food."

Once outside, he grabbed her hand in his, the paper bag in the other as they walked up to the front porch. There was something about him that made her stomach refuse to calm… not in a *I'm going to throw up* kind of way, but in a *dear God, who is this beautiful man* kind of way. It had been a long, long time since any man had interested her.

He unlocked the door and the lights came on as they stepped into the entrance. Light flooded an open space with beamed ceilings. "Keep the boots on, we're going outside," he said, tugging her along and into a massive kitchen. Everything was a combination of dark woods and steel. It was spotless. Endless windows and a peaked ceiling gave the kitchen an open, airy feel. The house wasn't enormous, but it was grand in a masculine, streamlined way.

He opened the massive, built-in stainless steel fridge and pulled out two beers. "I hope you like beer. If not—"

"It's fine," she said, holding out her hand. Fine. Why did she sound so stiff? Because she was stiff. She was waiting for him to become a jerk, or show signs of jerkiness. But he didn't. He was courteous and was now ushering her out the giant glass doors that led outside.

"Are you cold?"

She shook her head, following him down the lighted deck stairs. The smell of cedar and fall filled the heavy, nighttime air as they walked down at least two flights of stairs. The entire way down he held her hand, the other filled with beers and their dinner. When they reached the bottom, she forgot to breathe. Matt was walking around, but for once she wasn't admiring his beauty, but rather the view. They were perched high in the escarpment, secluded in the rawness of the pristine land around them. In the distance she could see twinkling city lights.

He had a fire lit in the massive fire pit and he took out a large, flannel, checkered blanket. He laid it down in front of the fire and then sat on the blanket and looked up at her. Her voice was trapped somewhere inside, maybe trapped by the same thing that was rendering her limbs useless. She should want to run from a setting this intimate.

"I know this is a far cry from Pasquale's. This is my own personal fortress. Safest place around." He said it with a smile that stirred her insides.

They opened each of their containers and ate at the same time. "Omigod," she said, trying not to moan out loud.

He handed her a beer and she shook her head. "Not yet. I can't let this taste leave my mouth yet," she said, trying to not inhale at a rate that would be completely embarrassing.

He took a long drink of his beer. "It's damn fine, artery-clogging food, isn't it?"

She nodded, her mouth full. "The best way to go."

"I can think of another but this would be my second."

She took a drink of the cool beer, and didn't look over at him. "I think I forgot my files on your kitchen counter," she said, not really knowing why she was bringing that up now.

"Huh. I guess I'll keep my innuendos quiet until I've charmed you a little more."

This time she laughed out loud. He finished his food, put the lid on, and dropped it in the paper bag. She did the same a few minutes later, her beer the only thing remaining. She looked at the label. He was stretched out on the blanket, lying back, bracing his weight against his forearms. It felt too suggestive to lie down beside him, so she sat cross-legged on the blanket.

"So, why don't you tell me about the fundraiser? In your words, without the papers."

Kate nodded. "We've already been approved by town council to open a small group home for mothers and their children escaping domestic violence. There is a regional shelter, but it's always over-capacity. This will be a small home, for sure, only able to accommodate up to four families. But it will be an intimate, safe, positive place for them to stay while they're getting their feet on the ground. There will be an in-house counselor who can even help with finding them training and placement for work if it's needed."

He stared at her for a long beat. "It's a good cause. How have donations been so far?"

"Generous. We were kinda worried in the beginning, thinking that maybe some of the residents wouldn't want a house like that in a residential neighborhood, but so far, nothing. Luckily, Still Harbor's mayor, Drew Weston, has backed this project."

"Ah, nothing like election time, right?"

"Exactly. So, the fundraiser should deliver the rest of the money we need for the remaining supplies and small repairs for the house. The fundraiser is in November."

"Women Abuse Prevention Month."

Feeling the wind pick up, the October air cooling, she wrapped her arms around herself. The crackling and popping from the fire pit was random and spontaneous, making her jump every now and then. But right now, she was preoccupied by how knowledgeable he was about the cause. "That's right."

"So what do you need? My sister was babbling about a major donor."

She laughed. "We'll be happy with whatever your

company can afford."

He named a figure that made her jaw drop and then he stretched out on the blanket, tucking his arms behind his head. Her gaze wandered the length of him, and then her mouth watered. But the biggest appeal was the donation. "That's really generous. Your donation will single-handedly put us in the black."

"Good. If there's anything else you need, let me know. Painting or repairs, whatever. Call my office tomorrow morning and we can figure things out."

"What is your office? I mean, I know you used to be a cop."

"I'm a PI."

"Oh."

"Usually, this is where someone would ask, 'why?'"

She smiled and shrugged. "I guess."

He turned on his side to look at her. She smoothed her hair, which was flying around with the wind. "Unless that person doesn't want me asking any return questions."

Huh. "That sounds about right."

He chuckled, his eyes crinkling at the corners, and he looked at her affectionately. "Usually, when people go on a date they try and get to know each other."

"True, but I think I remember saying that this wasn't a date."

"You're right, but then you wore the damn boots, and you totally look like you can kick my ass, which I find incredibly attractive. And you ate the poutine. And drank the beer. And you didn't pull out the mace. You sat out here in the middle of nowhere, not complaining at all that I didn't take you to a nice place for dinner."

She burst out laughing, trying not to make it sound like an insane laugh. He sat up, his expression changing. It changed in a good way. Well, in a way most of the female population would react to, but not in a good way for her. She was trying to resist the man. His gaze dropped to her lips and her mouth went dry. Her heart rattled frantically inside her chest. The palms of her hands grew sweaty, and she was basically incapable of saying a word when his hand gently cupped the nape of her neck. In fact, her kick-ass boots weren't helping her one bit at the moment. Her boots should be kicking her in the ass for not moving away from him. He was sitting face-to-face with her now, and she took in his features. His mouth in particular held her interest. It was sensual and seemed to always be ready with a smile. "I saw you the second I walked into the bar that night. I saw you and felt you were different."

His lips had moved so close to hers that if she edged forward a bit, his mouth would be on hers. "I'm actually not different," she said, hating that her voice sounded all breathy and nervous. "I'm similar to lots of people. I can even list off a bunch of people who look like me. And these boots aren't really kick-ass boots. I bought them because they were on the clearance rack."

A smile tugged at the corner of his mouth before his lips touched hers, and all her carefully constructed reasons as to why she'd never get involved with a man like Matt burned to ashes. He kissed her, explored her mouth with a soft, undemanding pressure. If she had wanted to, she could easily get up and walk away. His hand, bunched in her hair, held her with a light touch, but she couldn't have walked away from this moment. Hell, she wouldn't have been able to crawl away. Instead, she did the opposite—she leaned into him, craving him more than any emotional food binge. Right now, she could pretend there wasn't anything to be afraid of, that getting hurt wasn't a possibility.

Right now, she wanted to feel him, she wanted to feel his strength, she wanted the closeness he was offering. The second her mouth opened, his tongue slowly entered her mouth. She reached out to cling to his shoulders, feeling the hard muscles. He removed his mouth from hers and disappointment rocketed through her body, until she felt his mouth on her cheek, traveling to her earlobe, gently tugging, and then kissing the tender spot underneath. She tried not to weep like an affection-deprived adult woman, but good Lord, this man knew what he was doing.

He pulled back, his hand still at her nape. She tried not to fall forward or cry at the separation from this slice of heaven. "I thought I should stop. Don't want to be accused of wanting a quick screw." He smiled, a slow, sexy grin that demonstrated how in control he was. She shoved him, and he fell on his back with a laugh that made her toes curl.

"That's wise. I happen to know how to make serious threats."

"I know, and you don't put up with other people's crap."

"Well, you don't have to worry. I think you're safe for a while. First, you supplied me with copious amounts of artery-clogging food, then you donated more money than I ever could have imagined. So, I won't be doing any ass-kicking for now."

He laughed and it lured her in. She decided it was safe to lie down beside him on the blanket. It looked comfortable.

"Great, that's really nice of you. I feel much safer now."

She looked up at the sky over them. Stars were everywhere, lighting the night, destroying her theory that lying beside him wasn't intimate. It was. It felt as though they were the only two people in the world out here, and the stars were just for them. "This is the most gorgeous thing I've ever seen," she said, eyes fixed on the sky.

"One of the reasons I moved out here. It's worth the commute to the city. There are no stars in the city, no way to clear your head."

She turned to look at him.

He held on to her gaze for a long while, like he was looking through her, seeing all the things that were buried deep inside. "I know you're tough, and I know everyone's got shit in their past, some of us worse than others…"

She shook her head, trying to deny where he was going and the assumptions he was making. It was too soon.

"Let me finish, tough girl," he said, his voice softening. "I just want to tell you that I'm not one of the bad guys. And yeah, I get that people say that, but I'm not. Your cause, the women, the kids, it hits home. The first twelve years of my life I grew up in a house where my dad beat my mom and me. And then she took us and left. See, she's the best kick-ass woman I know. And we spent some time in one of those shelters, but it was crowded and in the city. My sister was two at the time. They helped my mom regain her confidence, helped her get a job, helped until we were able to move into our own apartment. I'm part of the white-ribbon campaign. I took an oath. As a police officer I took an oath. As a man, I took an oath. I will never, ever raise my hand in violence or use my words to belittle a woman. So you're safe. Whatever it is you're running from, you're safe with me."

She knew he was staring at her, but she blinked back the moisture collecting in her eyes and kept her eyes trained on the sky above. Her chest was heavy with the weight of what he'd said. He'd been brutally honest and so beautifully sincere that she didn't know what to say. How could she hide from that, even if she wanted to?

"You don't have to say anything, I just wanted you to know," he said, in that low, gruff voice that turned off all her internal alarms. He shouldn't have been able to. No one, no man, should have been able to do that, especially after one evening. But she knew liars, and he wasn't one of them.

"Tell me when you want me to drive you home."

She swallowed hard and managed a nod, not taking her

eyes off the stars. She didn't even hope to see a shooting star. Right now, she was happy and safe in this place. She didn't even jump when she felt his large, warm hand envelope hers. As his fingers entwined with hers, she decided it was nice. It was nice to actually feel safe and protected. It was nice to trust someone.

Chapter Five

Matt leaned against the boardroom table and looked out at his employees. He'd finished his weekly check-in with everyone, and Liam was just wrapping up the items he'd wanted to address.

In less than a decade, he and Liam had started up this business and turned it into one of the province's leading resources for confidential, private investigation services. They were both former detective sergeants and had worked on the drug squad together. Their entire agency was only employed with handpicked former and retired police officers. Liam and Matt both loved their work. Matt knew it was his friend and this business that had motivated him to get his life back after the accident and the death of his marriage.

"One last thing before everyone gets up," Matt said. He pulled out the jar that was on the table behind him and held it up. "We're collecting donations for a worthy cause. There's a women's shelter being constructed in Still Harbor and they need money. I've already made a sizeable donation and I'd appreciate you doing whatever you can. The jar will be on the reception desk. You can also help out by purchasing tickets to their fundraiser gala. K' thanks everyone."

Everyone filed out and he pretended he didn't notice the way Liam was grinning at him. It was a stupid grin.

"Wow, that was fast," his friend said. His voice had an annoying ring to it.

Matt folded his arms across his chest and put on his best *don't-shit-with-me* face.

Liam smiled, clearly not giving a rat's ass what Matt's expression said. "One date and you're already running some charity for her?"

"I'm not running it. It's a good cause. Why don't you open your wallet and donate, you cheap-ass."

Liam snorted. "Yeah, will do, but first, I need to hear—"

"I don't discuss my personal life."

"Yeah, you do. I knew all the sordid details of your divorce."

"This is different. There's nothing sordid going on. In fact, there's nothing really going on." That was kind of true. He had no idea what the hell had happened to him the other night. The moment he'd laid eyes on Kate at that bar, dodging that gross pickup attempt, he'd been attracted to her. When she'd danced with him, and he'd felt her body against his, some other feeling hit him. It had been fleeting. He hadn't had time to place it before she'd gotten some scared look in her eyes.

But the other night he'd gotten to know her on an entirely different level, one that played with the feelings in his past. She had lured him in. The woman was tough, but so damn vulnerable it had taken everything in him not to ask her what had made her that way. He knew he'd never see her again if he pushed. So instead, he'd kissed her, because he couldn't resist. He'd wanted to kiss her at the bar too, but at his house, sitting next to him, drinking beer and insulting him...well, that had been an intoxicating combination he couldn't resist. And he'd pulled back much sooner than he wanted. It had taken everything in him to pull away from her, especially since she had kissed him back with the same desire he'd felt. But he knew again that if he demanded too much she'd walk. So he'd played it safe and kept it very PG.

Then he'd revealed shit about his childhood that he made a policy not to discuss with people. Not because he was emotional about it. He was over it, but he didn't like to be reminded of a time when the women in his life were defenseless. It reminded him of a time when he wasn't in control, when he couldn't defend them. But he had wanted her to know. He'd taken the first shot at breaking down the wall between them in the hopes it would allow her to trust him.

His phone vibrated on the desk. His mother's picture came on the screen. He stifled his groan. Not that he minded talking to his mother, but he knew exactly what this was about. His little sister had already blabbed about his date. It rang and rang.

"You're avoiding phone calls from Barb?"

Matt frowned at him. "No."

"I'll talk to her," Liam said, trying to snatch his phone. Matt beat him to it and shot him a dirty look.

Liam shrugged. "Hey, that woman makes the best chocolate chips cookies in the damn country. I will gladly sell you out anytime."

"Go away," Matt said, taking the call.

"Matthew Eric Lane, I have been trying to reach you all day."

"Hi, Mom." Matt resisted the urge to groan out loud. It was exactly what he'd suspected.

"I have it on good authority—"

"Sabrina is an authority on nothing."

"That you have gone out on a date with a wonderful woman. I am very pleased to hear this, Matthew. It's about time. I'm sure you remembered your manners."

"I'm not five."

"Now, don't go getting embarrassed, dear, I'm just trying to help. So. How did it go?"

Matt banged his fist repeatedly on his forehead and shut his eyes.

"I hope you're not banging your fist on your forehead. I still think that can cause brain damage."

He stuffed his hand into his pocket. "Mom, everything went well, and that's it."

"Well, are you going out again?"

"I don't know."

"Ask her, Matthew. Don't let a good one go."

"Yeah. I will. I don't want to push. She, uh, has a kid." Liam stopped at the door and made a strangling motion with his hands. Matt flipped him the finger and turned his back on him.

"Oh, your sister didn't tell me that." There was a long pause, and then whispering.

"Mom, is Sabrina there?" he asked, ready to hang up the phone. Honestly, his sister could drive him to drink with all her antics.

"She's busy with homework. I brought her a snack and she was catching me up on the latest. So, like I was saying, I know what it's like to be a single mom, and when I was all on my own, I wish I would have met a man like you, Matthew. You're honest—"

He pinched the bridge of his nose and looked down. "All right, I think we're done here. Love you, gotta get back to work."

"And modest."

"Bye Mom."

"Don't forget about Thanksgiving dinner! Invite her to our house."

"I'm getting another call. Love you."

He drew a deep breath, and then tried to decompress. He loved his mother dearly, they were close. In some ways, he'd been the other parent in the house and he'd been his mom's defender. He knew how tough she'd had to be in order to take herself out of the situation she'd been in. He had a lot of respect for single mothers, which was why he usually stayed away from those sorts of situations. The single mom thing was the other reason he hadn't pressed or called Kate back this week. Single moms were different. The rules were all different. He frowned, thinking about how this was getting more complicated.

"Man, why are you staring out that window like some teenager who can't get a date to prom?"

Matt flipped his friend the finger, and was about to verbalize what an idiot Liam was, when there was a knock at the door. He turned around to find Derek standing there.

"Matt, can I speak to you for a moment, please?"

Matt nodded, waving his friend inside the room. Derek had officially joined their team this week. Liam sat behind the table, face hunched over his Blackberry.

"How are things going, Derek?"

The older man ran his hands along his wide jaw and gave a slight frown. "Well, everything here is great. Good people. Looking forward to my first case. But I'm coming to you about a personal matter."

Matt crossed his arms. "Okay. Go ahead."

"The charity, the woman who runs it. You said her name was Kate Abbott?"

Matt paused for a moment, studied his friend's weathered face, noting the tension, the pronounced lines around his mouth. "Actually, I didn't say what her name was."

Derek gave a brief nod. "Right. I think I must've read about it in the paper. Are you involved with her...personally?"

Matt didn't take his eyes off him. "Define personally."

"Friends? Lovers?"

He forced his muscles to remain calm. He didn't like where this was going. He'd never been the type to respond to orders or demands. "Why?"

"I know her, from a long time ago, and you should be warned that she's not who she appears to be. Watch your back is all I'm saying," Derek said, his eyes taking on a hard appearance before he started walking toward the door. Liam was no longer looking at his Blackberry.

"Hey, man, wait. What the hell is that supposed to mean? You got something to say about her, say it." Matt didn't like games and he knew Derek didn't either. He didn't know what his friend was talking about, but he found himself getting defensive.

Derek turned around. "I'm looking out for you, son. I know that ex of yours betrayed you, and I'd hate to see you have to go through some bullshit because of a woman all over again."

Derek walked out of the room before Matt could say another thing. He leaned against the desk, not knowing what had just happened. Tension pulled at all his muscles. What the hell could Kate have done? And how the hell did Derek know her? Matt knew people; he knew how to read them. He could sniff out liars a mile away. But neither Derek nor Kate were liars. Derek was like family to him. He had been more of a father to him than his biological one.

"What the hell was that?" Liam asked.

Matt shrugged. He was pissed off. "I have no idea."

"What's the deal with this Kate woman?"

Matt mentally scrolled through their time together, all the little telltale signs that she was lying. Sure, he knew she was hiding something, but his instincts told him it was hurt. He knew why Liam was looking at him like he'd lost his mind. His buddy had been there every step of the way through his divorce. Hell, if it hadn't been for his idea to start up the firm, he didn't know what would've happened to him. The idea to start their PI firm had given him the motivation to get his leg back into shape and to put his wife's cheating behind him. But the scorching sting of betrayal wasn't something he'd soon forget and, obviously, Liam hadn't either. "There is no deal with her. She's just a single mom. She's Sabrina's teacher. I don't know what the hell that doom-and-gloom warning was all about. It's not like him."

"Do you want me to run a background—"

"No," he said. "I don't. I'm not going down that road. If she's got something in her past then she'll tell me. That's assuming this is going anywhere. I may never see her again anyway." Okay, so that part might have been a bit of a stretch, because he damn well intended on seeing Kate again, but he wouldn't do a background check on her. No way. He didn't need to rifle through her past, no matter what Derek had said about her.

"What the hell would that do anyway? It's not like if we did a check on Michelle before I met her, it would've told me she would eventually cheat on me with my partner."

"If you change your mind, let me know. It sounds like Derek really didn't like her."

Matt stared at his friend's concerned face. Yeah, it hadn't sounded good, but he was determined to not invade her privacy. Nonetheless, he would get some answers about her and Derek. He'd ask Kate about Derek Stinson.

• • •

Kate stared at the young barista with what felt like bloodshot eyes. All the girls had come down with a nasty cold this week, and she, Alex, and Cara had taken turns with the nighttime wake-ups. This was a week from hell. All the fundraiser stuff was happening, too, on top of her already heavy work schedule, including the debate team she led at Still Harbor High. They were gearing up for their first debate next month, which meant extra sessions after school. Their house was trashed and at this point she was ready to yell at the poor, unsuspecting barista to hurry the hell up and hand her the grande double-shot latte.

She glanced at her watch. Janie was at speech therapy next door, which meant she had enough time to grab a coffee and then go back in and do some marking. Two hours of speech therapy would give her the opportunity to get something done, while still being able to look through the one-sided glass and make sure Janie was doing okay. Easy. That's all she had to do. Oh, and not sit there thinking about Matt, or their date, or what had made her feel so comfortable with him. And kiss him. He had called twice this week, and she, being the coward that she was, had texted him saying it was a crazy week.

Finally, her drink order was ready. She snapped a lid on and spun around, crashing into the hard, tall wall, of…Matt. How was it possible to literally crash into the same human being repeatedly? And why was it always her doing the crashing? He looked down at her with a *busted* expression on his face. Of course she was busted, because they both knew she had been avoiding him. So, his smile, of pure male smugness should irritate her. It should not be making her think how good he looked when he smiled. *Nope. Not thinking about any of that.*

"In a rush?"

She started shaking her head, but then nodded. "I'm so behind. All three girls were down with some nasty cold this week. I've got a pile of essays to mark, paperwork I'm behind on for the fundraiser, debate team practices to set up, and I've got less than two hours to do it." She took a deep breath. "While Janie's next door at speech therapy."

He leaned against the counter, folding his arms across his chest. "Well, it's your lucky day then. I'm at your service."

It was wrong to think of all the ways this man could be of service—none of them included any of the items she'd just mentioned. He disarmed her. "I really need to get back to the therapist's and get started." She swung her bag around in an attempt to move away quickly and make her point, but instead, the *Frozen* backpack got caught on the Thanksgiving Day Blend coffee display, knocking the entire thing over. She closed her eyes for the briefest moment, hoping that maybe it was all a dream. She opened them again to see Matt, crouched down, picking up the packs of coffee. She kneeled down beside him.

"I think you need a break," he said with a warm smile.

She started stacking the coffees in the display. "Or less caffeine."

"Why don't I come with you? There's got to be something I can help you with."

"I'm sure you have work to do. It's only four thirty."

"I'm done early. I needed to be somewhere at four this morning. I've done my time for the day," he said, standing and holding out his hand for her. She accepted it and rose, quickly pulling her hand back and reaching for her coffee. "C'mon, I promise, it'll be strictly work."

Ten minutes later they were settled at the small table outside Janie's room and she was unloading the backpack, Elsa's smirk taunting her. Their coffees were perched on the window ledge and Matt was staring through the window with a soft expression on his face. She didn't want to acknowledge she thought that was sweet.

"How's Janie doing?"

She divided her marking into two piles and then glanced up at him. "Really well. She's making huge progress." She abruptly stopped talking. She had been about to tell him that when she'd first met Janie, she hadn't been able to speak one word. That she hadn't started walking yet. That she had been delayed on almost every developmental milestone and that, while that was acceptable for children with Down's, with a little extra effort, she would be capable of achieving them. But she didn't say any of that. Instead, she looked away from the flicker of disappointment in Matt's eyes, and then down at her papers. She couldn't let him in. Yes, he'd opened up to her on their date, but that didn't mean she could do the same. She had known him for what, a week?

He stretched his long legs out to the side, crossed them at the ankles, and took a sip of his coffee. "Use me."

She tore her gaze from his great fitting jeans to meet his eyes. Even worse. They never showed irritation with her, even when she was irritated with herself, and the corner of his mouth was tilted up, like he was imagining all the naughty implications of his two words. She cleared her throat and picked up a stack of papers, tapping them on the desk until they were shuffled into a neat pile.

"C'mon. There's got to be something I can do."

She eyed him as she sipped her coffee. Why did he want to do this for her?

"Stop thinking of what ulterior motives I could possibly have."

Her brows snapped together. "How did you know that?"

"I told you what I do for a living. I'm also an expert at reading women. And even though you're a tough one, you're easier to read than you think."

Heat scorched its way up her neck and she placed her coffee down on the table. She didn't know if she should laugh it off or be upset, because he was right. She crossed her legs. "Fine. That's exactly what I was thinking. Why on earth would you want to sit in this tiny waiting room and help out with boring paperwork while I wait for my kid to finish her therapy?"

He leaned forward. Blue eyes darkening, mouth close to hers. She swallowed hard and met that gaze. "Because I liked our night together. Because I like you. Because I like everything I think you stand for." Just when she thought she wasn't going to be able to ever breathe normally again, he leaned in closer and this time his gaze went to her mouth. "And because I can't forget the way your mouth felt against mine."

She shut her eyes for a moment and then pulled back abruptly. She folded her hands on top of her stack of papers and forced herself to look at the incredibly hot man who had just spoken in a throaty, deliciously sensual voice about all these things that he liked about her. She tried to speak, but her vocal chords weren't working. She cleared her throat. "While I think those are all valid reasons—" She paused while he laughed. "It doesn't exactly mean you and I can go anywhere."

"Anywhere as in a relationship? Or out to dinner?"

She pinched the bridge of her nose. She should have known he wouldn't let her off easy. She could have said "ditto" after his statement. She had a feeling she liked him and what he stood for. And she couldn't forget the way his mouth felt either.

"Kate?"

She looked up.

"I told you a helluva lot of personal stuff about me, crap I don't share with most people. I'm a guy. Maybe not the best guy out there, but I'm a guy with a mother and a sister and, at the very least, I have to be the type of man I'd approve of either of them dating. I get you've been through a lot.

Sometimes you have to trust your gut and go with it, and I think if you listened to your instincts, you'd know I'm safe."

She blinked once, slowly, letting his words sink in. She couldn't be afraid her entire life. She needed to move on. And how often had she met a guy like him? She never trusted anyone this soon, and no one had ever managed to stimulate all her senses like Matt. She drew a shaky breath. "Okay, Matt." She didn't know what "okay" meant or what they'd do next, but his smile made her clutch her coffee cup tightly.

"Show me what I can do to help with this stack of work."

• • •

An hour and a half later, Matt was finishing the last tax receipt for the fundraiser donations, when the door opened and little Janie came running out. Kate swooped her up into a big hug and looked up at the young woman who was standing with her.

"How did it go?" Kate asked. Janie peered at him over Kate's shoulder and he gave her a wave and a smile. She immediately smiled back at him.

"Janie did awesome today. She was so focused, great progress. I'll see you next week, okay, Janie?"

Janie stood and turned to look at the woman. "Okay, Miss Katrina."

Once Miss Katrina left, Kate turned to Janie. "Do you remember Matt?"

Janie nodded. "Mr. Zibbits."

Kate turned some weird shade of purple and she was shaking her head slightly wildly. That Zibbits character again. He was going to have follow up on that, and he was going to have to curb his own jealous reactions before he scared Kate off. "No, no. This isn't Mr. Zibbits, sweetie. This is *Matt*."

She frowned at Kate and then turned to smile at him

again.

"So are you ladies hungry?"

Kate paused while collecting all the papers. "Well..."

"Yes. So hungry," Janie said.

Kate shoved the rest of her papers in the kid's backpack. "Matt, don't you have to get back to...something?"

He shook his head. "Nope. Nothing."

Janie thought that was funny. She gave him an adorable laugh that made him smile.

Kate sighed. "I had thought about going to that new sandwich place..."

"Great. I love sandwiches. Do they have fries?"

She nodded and then stood, about to swing the backpack over her shoulder when he grabbed it.

She raised an eyebrow. "You're going to carry the pink *Frozen* backpack?"

Janie slapped her hands across her mouth and laughed.

"I'm comfortable enough with my masculinity to wear this. Besides, I love Elsa," he said, winking at Janie.

Kate rolled her eyes, but she couldn't hide the gorgeous smile on her face. "Really? You watched *Frozen*?"

"My sister and mother are Disney buffs. Sometimes they force me to watch that cra—" He shot Janie a look, realizing she was listening raptly. "Crazy, hilarious movie."

Kate laughed under her breath and grabbed her purse. She took Janie's hand in hers and the three of them made their way out the front door. They walked the two blocks to downtown Still Harbor until they reached the Sandwich Hut. Matt held the door open and they walked through, settling at a table close to one of the front picture windows.

Once their orders were placed, Matt tried to get to know Janie a little better. "So how do you like first grade?"

Janie was silent for a moment, her brown eyes locked on his. "I like it. It's fun, and my teacher is really nice." Her words came out almost clear and he could read the pride in Kate's expression as she watched her little girl.

He hadn't heard Janie speak more than a few words in the two times he'd met her. Her voice was soft, and he could hear the slightly muffled, slurred pronunciation of her words.

"I liked first grade too," he said. He took in the mother and daughter in front of him. Not for the first time, he wondered what made Kate tick. She was fiercely protective of Janie, and he knew that a lot of that must come from bullshit she had to deal with when it came to the Down's syndrome. He didn't know much about it, and there was no way in hell he'd risk asking Kate until she trusted him more, in case she took it the wrong way.

Janie was now coloring, her brow furrowed, her brown hair held off her face by some cute cat hair clips. There was no way around it—the little girl was cute. He looked over at Kate. She was studying him, waiting for him to screw up, or show the tiniest hint of annoyance. He leaned back in his chair. Not going to happen.

As much as he hated to admit it, Derek's warning about her was playing in the back of his mind, but nothing this woman did or said sent off warning bells. There was nothing dishonest or sketchy about her. And hell, the last thing he wanted to do was mention Derek. For now, he'd rather risk being wrong than having her walk away from him.

"So, did you tackle a bunch of your grading?"

She nodded, her expression softening slightly. "I did. Thanks for the help with the tax receipts. You just saved me almost two hours of work tonight."

"No problem."

Their food arrived and Janie stared down at her grilled cheese, her forehead crinkling. Kate cut the sandwich into four pieces and added a small glob of ketchup on the side of the plate.

"Your sandwich looks good," he said once Janie started eating.

Kate took a bite of hers. "It's delicious. Grilled vegetables and goat cheese on a ciabatta. Delish. I see you're not very adventurous when it comes to food?"

He grinned and took a bite of his BLT with a side of fries. At least his sister wasn't here and he had half a chance of actually eating the fries today. "Nope. I save adventure for the real stuff. Bacon and fries, I don't need more than that."

He spotted Janie looking longingly at his fries. He pushed his plate closer to her and she looked up at him, all big eyes and hopeful smile. He nodded. "Go ahead, sweetheart." Then he looked over at Kate, who he'd have expected to reprimand him. Instead, she was eyeing his fries and eating her vegetable sandwich. Women. He gestured with his hand to the fries. She shook her head and pointed to her sandwich.

"Oh, thanks. Nope, I'm okay."

"I know you missed out on that platter of fried food at the bar that night." He paused while she choked on her food.

"It wasn't all for me, I was planning on sharing."

"Have some fries, Kate."

He watched her internal battle play across her eyes.

"They're soooooo good, Mommy," Janie said, poking her in the shoulder with one, complete with ketchup on it.

"All right," Kate said, taking one, popping it in her mouth, and blotting the ketchup off her sweater. He sat back with his BLT and let them inhale the rest of his fries until they got to the last two and Kate held Janie's hand back.

"Omigod, Matt. We ate all your fries. Here, you have the last two," she said, shoving the plate at him.

He took a long sip of his ice tea, trying not to laugh. "It's fine. You two finish them off."

Janie nodded. "Thank you."

He enjoyed spending time with them, with Janie, more

than he would have thought. Sure, he never really had a problem with kids, but he'd never hung around them since his sister had been little. The relationships after his divorce hadn't really been anything with depth, he hadn't wanted that. And yet here he was, sitting across from a woman and her kid that had somehow made him crave things he'd long ago dismissed as silly, unrealistic dreams of his youth. Kate was the whole package, and then some. He knew getting involved with her wouldn't be simple, or easy, and he knew he hadn't even scratched the surface of what this woman was all about. But right now, he knew he liked the way they made him feel, and he liked making them smile, even if it meant giving up his fries.

Janie was holding the last fry to her lips when she waved. He turned to see who he was waving at, and every nerve in his body snapped to attention. Two little girls and a mother and father stood in line. The two little girls blatantly ignored Janie's greeting and made nasty faces at her. He turned to Janie and watched as her innocent little face crumpled. Kate leaned down and smoothed her hair and whispered to her. The parents avoided eye contact with them and turned around, not even bothering to reprimand their kids.

No freaking way. Maybe it was Janie, or maybe it was just the pure cruelty at what the girls had done, and the mother who'd witnessed it and hadn't corrected her children's behavior, but ignorance wasn't an excuse. And hell if he wasn't going to stand up and—

"Matt, what are you doing?" Kate hissed, tugging on his shirt.

He had been trained to stand up for people, to defend. There was no way in hell he was going to let Janie be a victim of this. "I'm going to talk to those parents."

"No, they go to the same school."

"Even worse," he said, walking over there.

He was vaguely aware of Janie and Kate leaving as he walked up to the dad. He'd make this short and to the point, and then he'd go and chase down Kate. He tapped on the guy's shoulder, forcing himself to calm down as the man turned to face him.

"Not sure if you're aware, but your kids were making faces and rude gestures at a little girl sitting at the table over there."

The man didn't even blink. "I didn't see anything."

Matt rubbed his hand over his jaw. "Yeah, yeah, you did. Both of you did," he said, looking at the man's wife. She lifted up her chin and crossed her arms.

"You know how kids are."

"I do. That's why it's up to adults to correct inappropriate behavior."

The man frowned, his face turning red. "Are you saying my kids are rude?"

"I'm saying your kids are rude, and it's up to you to correct their behavior."

Kate was going to kill him. What the hell was he doing? He was creating a scene just like Kate hated. But he couldn't stand it. Janie's hurt face was stamped in his memory. The man took a step into him and Matt held his ground, aware that they had now drawn the attention of the entire restaurant.

"Hey, watch it."

He took a step into the father space. "*You* watch it. Make sure you speak with them about showing that little girl the respect she deserves."

People were idiots. He had no tolerance for idiots. Now that he wasn't a cop anymore, he didn't have to exercise patience around idiots—that had always been one of his weaknesses.

He bolted out of the restaurant and caught up with Kate as she marched down the street like a soldier, tugging Janie along with her.

"Kate!" he yelled out, a few passersby turning to look up at him. Kate ignored him, but Janie turned around to wave. He was relieved to see she didn't look upset anymore. He jogged and caught up to them. "Hey, stop."

Kate halted and frowned up at him. They were standing in front of her car. "Janie, sweetie, say thank you to Matt and let's get in the car."

"Thanks, Matt," she whispered. Of her own accord, she wrapped her arms around his leg. He leaned down to give her a proper hug, something inside his throat catching as she wrapped her little arms around his neck.

"You're welcome, sweetheart. Next time we'll share another plate of fries."

She pulled back and beamed at him, before Kate ushered her into her booster seat. Once Janie was buckled in, Kate handed her a book, shut the door, and turned to glare at him.

"You're pissed at me."

She crossed her arms and looked up at the sky. He had a feeling he'd be waiting a helluva long time for her to look down again if he didn't say something. "Kate, I was only trying to help."

She met his gaze, but her eyes weren't particularly warm. "Thank you, but we're fine. You don't need to help us."

"Really? 'Cause from where I was sitting, it looked like you needed help. Your little girl was sitting there confused because Thing One and Thing Two wouldn't give her the time of day and, sweetheart, you were wearing your heart on your sleeve. So, you know what? I was pissed for you and Janie. Forgive me for teaching some ignorant people something about human decency and common courtesy."

Her head looked like it was ready to blast off into space,

and she was tapping her foot and probably contemplating using her kick-ass boots to kick his. "No, it doesn't work like that. I don't know what you told those people, but all you did was succeed in shaming them into being nice for the moment. People don't change, their opinions don't change. Janie will have to deal with that forever."

"Yeah, and you should be teaching her how to be strong enough to defend herself."

"Excuse me?" She took a step closer to him. "Where do you get off telling me how to raise my daughter?" Her chin gave a slight wobble and he knew he was an asshole.

He held up his hands. "I'm sorry. You're right. I know nothing about kids, nothing about raising a kid who is different. Nothing about parenting."

"I can defend myself. I can defend my daughter," she said, her voice breaking. "I'm not *afraid*. I was just choosing to walk away." Her hands were clenched by her sides, her face red, and her eyes filled with tears. There was something else going on here, with her, with her reaction to all this. She was visibly shaking, tension transforming her into a very different person than the one he'd gotten to know.

He kept his gaze on her, needing her to relax, wanting her to smile. "Kate, I'm sorry."

Her shoulders relaxed slightly and she backed up a step. "I should get going."

"Hey, Kate? I wanted to see you, to get to know you and your daughter. I'm used to being the guy who steps up and defends. Occupational hazard. I speak my mind and I defend my friends. I get that you're used to doing it all on your own. Hell, I admire it."

She looked down at her boots, then up at the random people walking by. It was dark now, what was left of the warm fall day gone, replaced by damp, chilly air. After a silent minute, he didn't think she was going to speak. He stood there, hands in his pockets, wondering why it felt like he was sinking in thick, heavy quicksand. Finally, Kate raised her head and took a step closer to him. He clenched his hands, because he wanted more than anything to pull her into him, kiss her like he had the other night, and fight all her battles for her, but he needed to earn her trust first.

"My life is complicated, this is why I don't date. I know you were trying to help, I do. And if this, us, were actually going to go somewhere, I'm sure I'd even appreciate it. But we're not. I'd drive you crazy, Matt."

"You do," he said, swallowing up the remaining space between them. His back was to the car, and he could see she was periodically checking on Janie. "You drive me crazy in all the damn good ways that keep me up at night," he whispered. He cupped her jaw, his eyes going to her mouth. He could see her pulse racing at the base of her neck and she didn't move away when he bent his head. "The best ways, Kate," he said and then kissed her like he'd wanted to since the moment she'd ran into him that afternoon, since the moment she'd left him the other night. He kissed her, tasted her, wrapped her up in his arms, and tangled his hands in her hair until he couldn't think.

Until the sound of knocking made them pull apart. He turned around toward the car and they burst out laughing as Janie pressed her face against the glass.

Kate jogged away, toward the driver's side of the car. "I gotta go. Thanks for dinner."

He let the cool fall breeze wash over him and then did something he remembered so well from his youth, something he hadn't thought of or done in years, since his sister had been little. He blew Janie a kiss, smiling as she did the same. He put his thumb at the tip of his nose and did a side wave with his hand, and that earned him an earnest laugh before Kate drove away with a slight smile on her gorgeous face.

Chapter Six

Kate fumbled around in her purse, searching for her phone as it vibrated somewhere in that black hole. She was standing in line with the girls and Alex and Cara, waiting their turn for the carousel ride. It was the first county fair any of them had ever attended. They'd found out after living in Still Harbor for a year that the fair was a huge deal. It ran for almost an entire week, and there were horse shows, livestock competitions, contests, food exhibits, and an amusement park. They had promised the girls that they'd attend. It was a gorgeous autumn day, warm with a light breeze. They were going on hour number four and had promised one more ride before they went home.

She glanced down at the display on her phone: *so, do I need to volunteer more of my services in order to see you again?*

Matt. She tried not to smile, or look as though a giant tremor ran through her. Cara and Alex were stealth at deciphering if something remotely interesting was happening with her. He had called her a few days after their dinner and she wasn't so petty that she couldn't admit she was thrilled he'd called her. She told herself she could be thrilled, but she didn't need to act on that feeling. So she hadn't called him back. That was rude, and chicken of her.

And if she were being totally honest with herself, which she sometimes avoided, he had gotten close, closer to her and Janie than any other guy had. Despite being royally pissed that he'd interfered at the restaurant, she had also been touched. No guy had ever gone to bat for her, regardless of whether or not he'd been right, and that in and of itself brought forth another problem. Had Matt been right? Was she just chicken? Was she the same little girl who had been silenced? Should she have been the one to get up, fearless, and confront those people?

She stared down at the lit screen, and bit her lower lip wondering if she should answer. *Of course you should. Answer. He's a good guy. He's a hot guy. Answer.*

She quickly typed a reply. *No, but you might have to get me more poutine.*

Omigod, she'd broken out into a sweat just typing that. It was because her sisters were staring at her. That was why. Alex tried to snatch her phone. Another *gu-glink* sounded, and Kate stared at her screen, turning her back.

Consider it done. Where are you?

Hmm. That sounds kind of stalkerish.

No. If I were a stalker, I would have said, great, I'm watching you right now from the bushes.

She laughed out loud.

"Omigod, you're sexting," Alex whispered in her ear.

Kate glared at her and held the phone to her chest.

"Come on, we're almost next," Cassandra said, pushing them up the line like they were a herd of cattle. Sure enough, they would make it on the next carousel stop.

"I'm not. I just need to answer this. It's for work."

Alex scoffed. "I've seen the teachers you work with. I know it wouldn't create that blushing and frenzied typing."

Kate ignored her. She needed to get this text out before the carousel. *I'm at the county fair.*

Great. I love fairs.

Liar.

Sort of. Never been to one.

She wasn't going to laugh out loud again.

Yup. And rides. I'm about to go on a carousel right now.

How bout I meet up with you? One hour?

Kate chewed her lower lip.

"Say yes," Cara whispered, reading over her shoulder. Kate frowned and looked down at Cara's boots. "I should have worn heels, then you wouldn't be able to read over my shoulder."

Alex nudged her. "Seriously. Do it. Say yes…" She looked at the girls. "We'll take the girls home after—or to that cattle show over there—and you two can have time alone. Besides, you will never again score another man as hot as…Zibbits."

Kate shot her a dirty look, and then typed. *Okay. Five o'clock. I'll meet you at the Ferris Wheel.*

See you, TG.

TG. Tough girl. She was not internally smiling at the nickname.

"Who's TG?"

She glared at Alex. "Omigod, when did you become such a spy?"

A rapid tugging on her T-shirt reminded her they weren't in high school discussing boys and dates, not that that had ever been their lives, but at the moment that's what it felt like. She looked down to see Janie staring up at her anxiously.

"It's our turn," Janie said, pointing at the teenager who was motioning for them to get on.

"You're right, let's go," Kate said, taking her hand, glad to have an excuse to collect her thoughts. The girls all decided they needed to ride on black horses, so after much walking around the retro carousel, they were each in different areas. She helped Janie onto the horse, smiling as her daughter squealed, even though the ride hadn't started yet. She gave her a kiss and stood to one side of the horse, holding onto Janie's waist. The ride started with a gentle jostle and soon they were turning, the amusement park passing before them, the wind gently lifting their hair, the music dancing around them until all Kate could do was enjoy this moment. It was moments like this that made her so thankful for everything. She squeezed Janie's waist gently and kissed the top of her head, inhaling the sweet smell of her strawberry shampoo.

She would be meeting Matt in less than an hour. Matt. She hadn't been able to get him out of her mind all week. She glanced down at her clothes and closed her eyes briefly. Not exactly Tough Girl clothes today. No, today she was wearing sneakers with neon pink laces, worn jeans, and a pink T-shirt with a pink sweatshirt tied around her waist. Of course, she was wearing this candy-colored ensemble because Janie had begged her to wear the same colors she was wearing. Hm. Alex was dressed all in black. Maybe she should ask her to swap clothes. Black would be a better image, but that would mean infinite amounts of teasing. And her hair. She was wearing an SHH baseball cap. Well, whatever. The man was coming to a county fair. It was casual.

How good could he possibly look?

Hot.

Good God, Mr. Zibbits looked delectably scruffy, leaning against the wire fence. He was wearing jeans that were worn in all the right places, a T-shirt with the University of Toronto logo, and sunglasses. The shirt was tight around his chest and biceps, but loose over his stomach. And he was currently smiling. It was a smile that could stop traffic.

"You are indebted to us forever," Alex whispered as all six of them walked over to the man, like some messed-up, all-female version of the Brady Bunch. "We gave up that man for you. Just handed him to you on a platter, while we were forced to scarf down mounds of fried food and watch."

Kate couldn't reply without risking Matt hearing, but she agreed completely. She owed them.

"Look, Auntie Kate, your friend is here!"

Matt walked over to them, and she tried not to stare at his slight limp. So she hadn't imagined it the other night. She quickly went over to say hi, noting how awkward it felt since…they weren't really anything. They were friends who kissed each other at the end of their visits.

"Hi, ladies," Matt said with a warm smile.

And then they were all blabbering about a mile a minute, engaging him as they told him about the fair. She and Janie stood together. She knew Janie would have a hard time keeping up with the rapid pace of the chatter, plus all the noisy distractions around them.

"So we'll get going," Cara said. "And Janie, why don't you come back with us, honey?"

"I was thinking we could hang out with Janie for a while,"

Matt said.

Kate was surprised and didn't know what to do. She looked from the sincerity in Matt's blue eyes down to her daughter. Janie was smiling up at him as though she liked the idea.

"Why don't we do this? We'll hang out and get something to eat and then meet back here in an hour and take Janie home. That'll give you guys time to check out the fair and then have time," Cara's eyes shot between her and Matt, "for just the two of you."

What was wrong with her? Kate was a take-charge woman. So why was she letting everyone make all these plans for her? Because Matt had floored her. He could have easily agreed to Janie going home right away. Instead, he'd made the obvious attempt to get to know her even more. That went a hell of a long way.

"That sounds great," Kate finally said. "We'll meet you back here in an hour."

"See you, ladies," Matt said, grabbing her hand. Janie was already holding her other hand and the three of them made their way across the field and back toward the entertainment section.

"So this is a county fair. Never been to one of these things."

"Neither have we, but it's fun. The girls had a great time," she said, squeezing Janie's hand.

"What was your favorite thing today, Janie?" Matt asked, looking over at her. Janie looked up at him and then pointed to the booth with giant stuffed animals dangling off the side.

"I like unicorns."

"Janie is kind of obsessed with unicorns and we blew almost twenty dollars trying to win one."

"I'll win one."

"But it's impossible to win. They are rigged so people

keep spending money."

They approached the counter and Matt slapped down a twenty-dollar bill. Toy rifles were lined up and only a few were taken by other patrons. Janie started jumping up and down. Kate shook her head. This was going to be trouble, maybe even a full-blown meltdown. The poor girl was going to be disappointed for the second time today.

Matt positioned himself behind the rifle and Kate refused to acknowledge the incredible display of flexing muscle as he aimed. Fired. Bull's-eye. Once, twice, and three times.

"Omigod," Kate said as he straightened up, and gave her an incredible smile.

The teenager must have been shocked too, because he was scrambling with words when he came over, gave Matt his change and told him to pick whatever animal he wanted.

Matt kneeled down to look at Janie in the eye. "You pick, sweetheart."

"The pink unicorn," she said.

"Pink unicorn please," Matt said, straightening up. Kate looked down at Janie and refused to get all emotional, but the look in her daughter's eyes as the giant stuffed pink unicorn, with the furry white horn, was handed to her would be imprinted in her mind forever. The unicorn was almost bigger than Janie and, when she hugged it with enough force, she almost toppled over.

"What do you say, Janie?" Kate asked, swallowing the lump in her throat.

Janie moved the unicorn in order to look at Matt. "Thank you, Mr. Zibbits."

Kate coughed and placed her hands on Janie's mouth for a moment. "No, this isn't Mr. Zibbits, honey."

Matt gave her a pointed look. "Speaking of Zibbits, I'm going to ask you about him later." He reached out and tussled the top of Janie's head. "You're welcome. Now how about we get some food?"

Janie nodded and Kate forced herself to put aside the feelings that were running rampant through her body. She needed to process them in private. She needed to analyze him when he wasn't around flashing grins, and spewing "sweethearts" from his mouth.

"How did you manage that?" Kate asked as they began walking toward the food stands.

"I've had a bit of experience. Before I quit the force."

The police force. Right. Well, she was a grown-up and she knew she couldn't live in the past where everything was black and white. Just because she had been let down by an organization that was supposed to protect her, didn't mean all cops were the same. She felt he was one of the good guys.

Janie abruptly stopped walking.

"I want to go do that contest," Janie said, tugging on Kate's hand. They looked over at where she was pointing. Kate frowned as she stared at the three-legged race contest. It was another one of those moments where she struggled between wanting to let Janie do anything and wanting to keep her safe. She didn't want to limit her—she wanted her daughter to grow up believing she could do anything—but this was beyond her. That wasn't being pessimistic, just realistic.

"Well, we were planning on getting some food now, Janie. Matt already got you the unicorn. Why don't we take a break from all that stuff?" She held her breath, hoping Janie would go for her explanation.

Matt read the sign out loud. "It says kids can choose a partner, the only requirement is that it's fair play, open to all ages."

Janie started walking ahead of them. "I don't know," Kate whispered as they followed behind Janie. "She's usually not this extroverted."

"Looks fairly tame. We're right here, we'll watch her."

"If only Cassy and Beth were still here. One of them could've partnered with you, sweetie," she said, leaning down beside Janie. They were in the crowd full of people getting ready.

"I want to," Janie said.

Kate nodded after a minute. She was going to have to learn not to be so over-protective.

"I'll sign her up, you help her get ready," Matt said, already walking over to the registration table.

Janie had no fear and walked right into the crowd of children. Kate stood a little off to the side, close enough that she could hear what was happening, but far enough that Janie had her independence. She crossed her arms and watched as the children one by one began pairing off. One of the event coordinators, a young woman, addressed the crowd of children. "Okay kids, the race is about to start, so find your partner and then come up to the starting line where we'll help you into the burlap sack."

Panic stomped on any ounce of excitement Kate had when the last two girls were Janie and another little girl who looked around her age. Matt joined Kate, but she couldn't even look over at him, her eyes were glued on the two kids.

"What's up?"

"She's going to reject her, Matt. I'm going to go over and pull—"

He grabbed her hand in his and squeezed. "You don't know that," he whispered.

She nodded and it literally felt like her heart crumpled into a thousand pieces as the little girl backed away from Janie and went to stand with her parents, who did nothing to stop her. She heard Matt swear under his breath, and before she knew what was happening, before Janie could figure out what had just happened, he was by Janie's side. He kneeled down, said something to her. She nodded vigorously and held his hand. To the starting line. What was he doing?

She watched as he spoke to the coordinator, watched as the young woman fell to his killer smile and then melted in front of him, handing him some rope and a sack. He was going to do the race with Janie. He spoke to Janie, and she nodded, her tongue protruding slightly as she listened, her eyes focused on the course in front of them. They leaned down a little. Kate smiled as Janie tried to copy Matt's position. Kate held her breath and waited, watching. She didn't miss the look Matt shot the dad of the little girl who'd walked away from Janie.

The starting flag was raised and everyone was off.

The crowd cheered and everyone was yelling their kids' names as they made their way across the course. Kate was jumping up and down, and Matt and Janie were neck and neck with two boys. She could tell that Janie was leaning heavily on Matt, and one of her arms was clutching his leg, but he just grabbed on to her, his eyes on the finish line.

Kate let out a scream she had no idea she was capable of and threw her hands in the air as they broke through the yellow ribbon at the finish line.

Matt swooped Janie up in his arms and hugged her tightly. Emotion washed through Kate, pummeled over her in waves that held her down for a moment, making her feel as though she were drowning. She knew in that moment, watching him with her daughter—laughing, hugging her—that she felt something profound for this man. He hadn't let her daughter feel the biting sting of rejection. Twice. He'd defended them without thinking, while she'd stood on the sidelines, doing nothing.

He'd taken over, changed the situation. He'd defended Janie when everyone else had rejected her. Kate had spent her entire childhood waiting for someone to do the right thing, to help her mother, her sister. There was a time, before Derek, when she had believed in fairy tales and happy endings, believed that right would always win, that someone would save them, someone would believe her. And no one had. She had spent her entire adolescence avoiding people, relying on herself, trusting no one. She had given up on the idea that there were men with inherent decency in them. Until now.

Janie and Matt were walking toward her. Kate opened her arms and Janie came flying into her, almost knocking her down. "We won!" she screamed, holding out her ribbon. Kate squeezed her eyes shut, holding Janie, letting all the hope that had evaporated over time to trickle back in. Kate gave her not nearly as many kisses as she wanted before Janie was standing up with Matt again. He'd obviously won her daughter's heart as well.

She noticed with a small pang that his limp was back and he was favoring his other leg, probably because of hauling Janie along during the race, but he didn't say a thing.

"Okay, I think we need to eat."

"Yeah, Matt and I are hungry," Janie said, beaming up at him, as though he'd just given her everything she'd ever wanted.

Five minutes later they stopped in front of a food truck that was advertising the best poutine around. "Are you game?" he asked, tilting his head in the direction of the grease pit.

She smiled at him. "Definitely." She looked down at Janie. "Do you want fries, sweetie?"

Janie nodded. "Ketchup."

"Of course. Everyone needs ketchup," Matt said, walking up to order.

"Wait, I'm paying," Kate yelled, a little too loudly.

Matt looked around. "Nope, my treat."

"You already treated us."

"More treats."

She bumped her hip against his, trying to shove him, but the man was solid.

"Did you just hip bump me in an attempt to pay?"

She couldn't help but laugh.

"I asked you out, I'm paying. Besides, you need to watch Janie because she wants her unicorn to take a drink from that water fountain," he said, tilting his chin behind her.

Kate spun around. Sure enough, Janie was a few feet away and trying to guide her unicorn to take a dip into the water fountain. She ran up to her and gently reminded her she wasn't allowed to walk away, even if she had a unicorn, no matter how thirsty her unicorn claimed to be. "You can play with the unicorn at home. You can walk him around the backyard, okay?"

Janie nodded agreeably and Matt was already walking over to them with a satisfied grin, and a tray loaded with food. "I think there're a few picnic tables over by the horse show," he said, leading the way.

Kate looked down at Janie who was dragging her unicorn along, a strange feeling sweeping over her. Yes, she was happy, Janie was happy, and they were both here with Matt, a guy who hadn't run when he found out she had a little girl with Down's syndrome. He hadn't blinked an eye. He hadn't asked her a question at all, not even the obvious question people always asked. Every time someone asked her why, she would ask them why not, then watch them squirm as they realized how offensive their question was. So, what was the problem?

Her. She was the problem because she liked him too much. She was attracted to him in a way that scared her, because it was all-consuming. He wasn't just a good-looking guy. He was the entire package...and if she was wrong about that, if he turned out to be like all the rest, then she was gearing up for epic disappointment. And if things continued at this crazy pace, maybe even epic heartbreak.

They settled at a picnic table sheltered under one of the large oak trees and Matt began divvying up the food. She watched as though on the sidelines and tried to process what was happening here.

Matt smiled tenderly at her daughter. He nodded at something she said and helped her squeeze more ketchup on her fries. Then he turned to Kate and her breath caught for a second as he turned that affection toward her. Good God, Matt was winning them both over.

"Hey, first you demand poutine, now you're not even eating it," he said, smiling. He stabbed his fries with the plastic fork, shoving an indecent amount in his mouth, and he didn't even look gross doing it.

She forced herself to dump her thoughts and enjoy the moment. It was good for Janie to be around a man, to have that company. And who was she kidding? It was pretty damn good for her too. "I'm eating, I'm eating. I try and savor each bite instead of inhaling mine like a vacuum," she said, eyeing his almost empty paper container.

He laughed. "That makes sense in theory, but there's a lot of food around here. If you take too long eating that, you'll never have time to get dessert. I saw Beaver Tails. What's the point of going to a fair if you can't win unicorns and eat bad food?"

Chapter Seven

Matt waved good-bye to Kate's crew, while holding on to her hand. He was holding on to her hand partly because in the back of his mind he wondered if she'd take off with them, and partly because he wanted to. When he'd texted her before, it had been spur of the moment. Yeah, he knew he wanted to see her again, and yeah, he knew she was the type of woman who came with strings and ropes and all the other stuff that worked its way around him until he wasn't able to break free anymore.

He'd half expected her to be pissed at him for interfering the other night. The more he thought about it, the more he wanted to know everything about her. She had taken on a hell of a lot for a single, young woman, and he wanted to know why, and why it seemed like she was vulnerable, even though she acted courageously. And, of course, the other thing that kept bothering him and was never far from his mind was what Derek had implied about her.

"So..." he said, turning to look down at Kate. She was still focused on watching the kids and her sisters walk away, so he focused on the gorgeous site in front of him. She wasn't wearing the kick-ass boots today. She was softer looking, cuter, or maybe that was because her guard was finally coming down a little. She was wearing dark jeans that hugged her body so closely he was jealous of them, a pink T-shirt that showed off some awesome curves, and an adorable baseball cap. Bottom line, Kate was hot. "What do you want to do now?"

She finally turned to look up at him. "No more food."

He smiled and looked beyond her. "Ferris wheel?"

"Only if you promise not to make the seat swing crazily."

He laughed and tugged her hand gently, walking in the direction of the Ferris wheel. "I think you have the wrong impression of me. I would never do something like that." He wasn't going to tell her that he'd gotten himself kicked off a Ferris wheel when he was a teenager for doing that very thing.

Dusk had settled in, and the lights from the rides and vendors were glowing. They walked through the crowds of people. Every now and then Kate would tuck herself close to him in order to avoid a group of people who didn't know how to share communal space. He found himself craving the feel of her, her nearness, her softness.

They stood in line, close together. "I don't think I've ever been on a Ferris wheel," she said, looking up at him.

He tipped her hat up slightly, because he wanted to see her eyes. "Really? Are you afraid of heights?"

She shook her head. "Nope. I just…huh. Well, amusement parks are expensive. There wasn't a lot of disposable income growing up." She shrugged and then looked way up at the lit Ferris wheel, and again, he found himself wanting to know more, but he also knew she wasn't the type of woman to give up her secrets to just any guy. He was going to have to work for it, even if it meant telling her way more than he told most people.

"Yeah, we didn't have a lot. The first time I went to one,

I snuck in with a bunch of friends."

She gave him a mock gasp. "Weren't you a cop?"

He grinned. "This was long before those years. This was during the troubled teen years."

"Ah, yes. Who doesn't have those in their past?"

The teen manning the Ferris wheel opened up the barrier and it was their turn to walk through and get seated. He held the little door open for Kate and then settled in beside her. Her leg and thigh were pressed up against his and he tried to position his legs comfortably. His damn bad leg was having difficulty conforming to the odd angle and limited seating space necessary to make his legs fit in the tight space. It had also been throbbing like a sonofabitch since that race, but he wasn't going to say a damn thing about it. Tomorrow, he'd just book himself a session with the physiotherapist he still saw regularly, and hopefully that would set it straight. Right now, he wasn't going to let anything ruin tonight.

"Are you okay? Here, I can move over," Kate whispered, her voice filled with something that sounded like sympathy.

He didn't like sympathy, even if he liked the way her voice softened. "I'm okay. These things are a lot smaller than I remembered."

The teen jostled their safety bar until it clicked and then shut the door.

Kate looked at him, her eyes glistening with anticipation. "I think I'm way too old to be this excited about a ride."

"Never too old."

Neither of them said anything as they started their ascent, the view below them increasingly spectacular, with the twinkling lights and the crowds and the music. It was almost perfect. He placed his arm around her shoulder, felt her stiffen for the briefest of seconds, before relaxing against him. "You know what else happens on Ferris wheels, don't you?" he asked.

She turned to him, her gorgeous face a few inches from his. Her eyes went from his to his lips. She shook her head.

"People kiss at the top," he said, lowering his face to hers, his mouth hovering so close to those lips he'd been craving.

"Really?" she said softly, her tongue licking her lips. "Is that what you and your guy friends did when you rode the Ferris wheel together?"

He laughed against her mouth. "You're kind of a shit-disturber, aren't you, Kate?"

"Only when I'm being fed bullshit lines."

This time he stopped talking and kissed her like he'd wanted to the moment he saw her that afternoon. He tilted her hat up, his mouth not leaving hers as the Ferris wheel lifted them to the top and stopped. His tongue delved into her mouth, exploring, needing more of her. She made a soft, sexy moan and then her hands went to the nape of his neck and pulled him closer. Blood rushed through him and he forgot where they were, forgot everything except the need to be with this woman who intoxicated him on so many levels.

"Excuse me, sir," the teenager said in his ear.

Kate let out her own little squeal and ripped her mouth from his. "Omigod," she whispered in a frenzy of straightening herself out and pulling her cap low over her forehead.

"Yeah, hold on there, buddy," Matt said, needing a minute. "See, now you know why Ferris wheels are so popular," Matt said under his breath to Kate. He took her hand when they left their seat, wandering out in the crowd again. The lights from the rides and exhibits glowed, the air filled with the smell of food and autumn, as they strolled through the aisles.

"I guess I should probably call it a night," she said, gathering the sweater that was tied around her waist. She put it on and zipped it up. He didn't want her to go. Liam was right. He was acting like a damn infatuated teenager. He was at a fair, participating in events, going on the Ferris wheel.

There was something about her that made him not want to leave.

"I'll drive you home," he said.

She nodded and they started walking toward the parking lot.

"Do you have plans for tomorrow night?"

Gravel crunched beneath their feet and they stopped, being told to wait as a horse and buggy passed in front of them. Once they were walking again she answered. "Tomorrow is Pumpkinfest and we promised the girls they could each enter the pumpkin carving contest."

Pumpkinfest. "I love pumpkins."

Kate laughed, and he smiled at the sound. "You're full of crap, Matt."

"That's incredibly rude. I happen to be the best pumpkin carver in...all of Canada." He had never carved a pumpkin in his damned life. When he was small, his mother had done the pumpkin carving, while his dad had nothing to do with holidays. When they were older, and away from their father, they lived in an apartment. Now as an adult he had no need. It's not like he even got trick-or-treaters at his door. But if claiming he could carve a pumpkin could gain him another date with Kate, he'd do it.

They stopped at his SUV. She looked up at him, her eyes narrowed, and he could tell she was trying not to smile. "The only way I'll say yes to this is if you admit you're lying." She attempted to poke him in the stomach and he laughed, grabbing her hand and backing her up against his Range Rover. The lot was dark, mostly empty except for the occasional passerby in the distance. She didn't attempt to move as she stood pressed to him. He released his hold on her wrist, not wanting her to feel trapped. He wanted her to know she could walk away if she wanted. But she didn't. She grabbed a fistful of his shirt and pulled him in, like he needed any encouragement. He raised his hands to cup her face, feeling the anticipation course through her, as powerfully as it did in him. This time, when he took her mouth against his, he knew exactly how she'd taste, how she'd kiss him back, and he'd never forget. It was supposed to be light, and noncommittal, but he couldn't have Kate in his arms and not want more. There wasn't an ounce of air between them, which was how he always wanted it to be when he was around her.

Her hat was getting in the way so he tried to take it off, but she swatted him with her hands.

"Don't," she mumbled against his mouth. "I have hat head."

He laughed, moving his mouth to her neck, the sweet spot beneath her ear lobe. "I need better access, I couldn't care less what your hair looks like."

Headlights beaming in their direction finally made him slowly pull away.

"I want you," he whispered in her ear before taking a step back, feeling her shiver.

Her eyes were still closed, her lips swollen, but there was a faint trace of a smile.

She straightened out her clothes and then looked up at him. "Next week's kind of busy. The gala is in three weeks and there's Thanksgiving..."

"So that means no to Pumpkinfest. I make a mean pumpkin pie."

She angled her head and gave him a teacher frown. "No you don't."

"Well, I mean my mother does. And she makes the best turkey," he said with a shrug. Good God, he was inviting a woman to Thanksgiving with his mother and sister? This never happened. Hell, even when he was married, Michelle had rarely spent time with his family. There was something about Kate and Janie though. They brought out this—God forbid—softer side. Or maybe the selfless side in him that wanted to make them happy and safe.

"What are we doing here? What are you doing?" She was frowning and looking vulnerable all at the same time as she crossed her arms and slammed her hat back on her head.

What was he doing? He knew enough to know that whatever it was, it felt right.

"We're two adults who like spending time together."

"Why haven't you asked me why I adopted Janie?"

He frowned. Where was this coming from? His people-reading skills were finely honed, a combination of professional training and just his own instincts. She was waiting for him to say something, something that would incriminate him so she would have an excuse to walk away before things became serious. So he told her the truth and waited for the downfall. "Are you waiting for me to ask you why you would adopt a child with Down's syndrome?"

He kept his gaze on her eyes, seeing the shock register, her back straighten, her lips tighten. "That's just what people usually ask."

"Right, and I'm like usual people. See, I think you're setting me up to fail. I think you want me to be like the rest of them. I think you want me to be some asshole who thinks Janie is less than perfect. Janie is what she is. She was born to be the kid she's supposed to be. And you adopted her. That's it as far as I'm concerned."

"So I'm just supposed to believe that you accept her? You wouldn't be disappointed? It hasn't once crossed your mind that life with a child like her would be harder or—"

"Hey, I never said I was perfect. I'm sure as hell not. And if you and I had a baby together, and when that baby was born she or he wasn't what we expected? Yeah, I don't know what I'd think. I can't say because I've never been in that position, expecting one thing and getting another. I know enough about myself to know that I love what's mine. I don't walk away from what's mine."

Her chin was wobbling and her eyes were glassy, filled to the brim with tears that he knew she was holding on to for dear life.

He cleared his throat. "The only Janie I know is the one I've met. I've never imagined her in any other way than what she is right now. And she's a kid, a special little kid and that's good enough for me."

She opened her mouth and he guessed when she didn't speak that he had given her the right answer. He moved a step into her, loving how she didn't pull back, how she automatically leaned into him, even if she wasn't touching him.

"You don't have to be tough with me, Kate."

"This is happening too fast to be real. You can't be real," she whispered.

"Trust me, I'm very real. I'm not a saint, but I'm not an idiot. I've made a lot of wrong choices, stupid choices, but I learned from them. I'm old enough to know what I want from life, who I want in my life. If you think I'm some guy who runs the other way at the mention of a real relationship, then you got me all wrong. Maybe at first I wasn't looking for a relationship, but you reeled me in, sweetheart, and I'm not going anywhere."

He stopped, because she let out a breath as she tilted her head back and stared at the darkened sky. She was blinking back tears, still didn't say anything so he kept on talking. "It's okay to be soft once and a while. It's okay to need someone. You can trust me. I'll never take advantage of that," he said, his voice sounding gruff to his own ears as he pulled her into him. "But you can still wear the boots because they're pretty damn hot."

She laughed against his chest, hugging him back.

Chapter Eight

It's okay to be soft once and a while. It's okay to need someone. You can trust me, I'll never take advantage of that...

Kate slowly lowered her head to her desk, Matt's words echoing in her mind like a comforting blanket. The school day had ended thirty minutes ago and she was getting ready for a staff meeting before going home. She had to admit she'd been a bit disappointed when he hadn't called about Pumpkinfest on Sunday, but she knew he worked long hours and often on weekends. She couldn't get him out of her head. He was everywhere. His deep voice, his laugh, the feel of his hard body against hers...there was no denying she was falling for him. At some point he was going to demand more, he was going to demand some answers.

The only Janie I know is the one I've met. I've never imagined her in any other way than what she is right now. And she's a kid. A special little kid and that's good enough for me.

"You are so screwed," she mumbled against the stack of report cards.

"Miss Abbott?"

Kate jerked her head up at the sound of Matt's little sister's voice. She had thought she was alone. She felt her face going red as Sabrina stood there, looking a little embarrassed.

"Sorry, Sabrina. I was um, just thinking about—"

"My brother?"

Kate shuffled the report cards around on her desk, thinking that his sister was a lot like him—direct and to the point. She forced herself to look up at Sabrina with an expression of calm. The look in Sabrina's eyes told her she hadn't exactly pulled it off. "No, no this isn't about Matt. I was thinking about everything that needs to get done before Thanksgiving."

"Oh, so you haven't heard what happened to him?"

Kate's heart stopped for a moment. "Something happened? Is he okay?"

Sabrina waved a hand. "Oh yeah, he'll be fine. He hurt his bad leg so he hasn't been to work in two days which is, like, a record for him."

"What happened?"

She shrugged, but her eyes didn't leave Kate's face. "I dunno. It never fully got better after he was shot, but I think he might have hurt it over the weekend."

The image of him wincing in the Ferris wheel and then limping after the race with Janie popped into her head. She felt awful. He hadn't let on that it was that bad, but that had to be it, which would explain why he hadn't called her for Pumpkinfest.

"Thanks for telling me. I'll give him a call to see if I can do anything."

"Just don't tell him I told you or he'll be pissed. Oh, and don't act like you're all concerned or he'll totally pretend like there's nothing wrong," she said, backing away from Kate's desk, but not before smiling a little.

"Thanks for the tip," she said, rising from her chair and gathering her things. Sabrina left the room and Kate knew she'd have to go see him. She just needed to get through the meeting, then she would acquire caffeine for the drive, and then...go see Matt.

• • •

Matt swore out loud and then slammed his laptop lid shut. He hated feeling useless. Tomorrow he was going back to work even if it meant hobbling in there like an old man. He could have gone in and sat behind his desk for the past two days, but then that would have involved everyone asking why he was in his office all day. He hated calling attention to his old injury, and he'd been great at managing it, but this was a reminder that he wasn't back to his old self and he never would be. But there was a new case and a guy flying in from Vancouver just to meet with him. He wouldn't miss that tomorrow. Apparently, this man had fathered a child he hadn't known about and needed Matt's help tracking the kid down.

He limped out of his home office on the main floor and made his way to the kitchen. Rain streamed down the windows outside and pounded the deck ferociously, suiting his mood. He swung open the fridge and glowered in disgust. Beer, apples, milk. He wasn't eating cereal again.

The doorbell sounded and he made his way to the front door slowly. He wasn't expecting anyone, though there was one person he'd love to see on the other side.

He opened it—not her. Derek was standing on the covered porch, holding a six-pack of beer and an umbrella.

"Thought you could use some company," he said, walking in.

"Thanks, man, come on in." Derek handed him the beer while he shrugged out of his rain gear. Even though the guy was well into his sixties, he kept himself in great shape.

"So, how's the leg? Really."

Matt shrugged and started walking to the great room, Derek following. "Hurts like a sonofabitch, if you wanna know the truth." He didn't have to pretend. The man had seen him at his worst and he knew what these kinds of injuries were like. He sat opposite Derek and propped his bad leg up on the coffee table.

Derek leaned over, opened a beer, and handed it to him before grabbing another for himself. "How'd you hurt it?"

He looked down at the beer in his hand. He knew the exact moment—the race with little Janie. The kid had unknowingly put so much pressure on it, pulling it during the race, that it had triggered the muscle strain. And then he'd been too proud to tell Kate that the Ferris wheel had continued to kill it. "I was hanging out at the fair this weekend and did something stupid."

Derek gave a short laugh. "I can't picture you at a fair."

"Yeah, well, I went for the company." A part of him wanted to tell Derek about Kate. If it weren't for that comment he had made at the office Matt would have talked about her.

"Ah, a woman?" Derek asked, leaning back in the sofa.

Matt took a drink of the cold beer and studied his friend carefully. "Kate."

A tiny vein in Derek's temple strained slightly. "So, you're still involved with her?"

Matt shifted, eyes still trained on his friend. "Yeah."

Derek took a swig of beer. "I see what I told you had no impact."

Matt forced his muscles to relax, hating that this rift was forming. He had never doubted Derek once in all the years he'd known him, but he was defensive. "You didn't really tell me much of anything."

"Did you ask her about me?"

"No."

Derek shrugged and gave him a tight smile. "Well, let's stop talking about this anyway. I should get going."

"Do you want me to ask her about you?"

Derek stared at him, an expression in his eyes Matt couldn't quite make out. "Nah. No point. It was all a long time ago. I made too big of a deal about it, anyway. It's nothing. I wish her the best."

"I'm not sure I buy that. You told me to watch out."

"I'm just looking out for you. You're like the kid I never had."

Matt tried to relax his posture, to not be so defensive. "So seriously, everything's good? There's no issue?"

"Don't get serious. Get what you want and then move on."

Matt blinked. "It's not like that. She's not that kind of person. And she has a kid."

"What?"

Matt nodded. "She adopted a little girl with Down's syndrome."

He could have sworn Derek's face paled. "You really want to get involved in something like that?"

Ah, hell. "We should probably stop talking about this, unless you want to tell me what it is you've got against this woman."

"I know how Michelle hurt you. She kept secrets, she was dishonest."

"She cheated on me. She was nothing like Kate."

"You so sure about that? She's completely honest with you? You don't think she's hiding shit from you? Don't let yourself get distracted by a nice piece of ass."

"Watch it." Matt stood abruptly and swore as the fast movement caused pain to ricochet through his leg. "I think we're done with this conversation. I don't know what the hell is going on, but right now you're sounding like a prick and nothing like the man I know."

Derek stood abruptly, waving. "You're right. Maybe I'm just a jealous old man," he said with a laugh that sounded fake as hell. "We still on for Thanksgiving? Nothing like Barb's cooking. The only home-cooked meals I get."

Matt ran his hands down his face. What the hell *was* going on here? Liam's offer to run a background check on Kate drifted through his mind, even though he hated the idea of going behind her back. He hated what his friend was implying, but couldn't ignore his warnings either.

"Your mother makes the best stuffing and cranberry sauce," Derek said with a grin. Matt cringed. There was no way they'd all be spending Thanksgiving together this year. He took in Derek's gray hair, the deep lines etched in a weathered face. "I, uh, I have plans for the holiday."

He stood and they walked in silence to the front door. Awkward silence. Hell, men didn't do awkward silence. Things had never been like this with Derek, but it was there, this damn rift. Because of Kate. None of this added up. Derek had never been anything other than a great guy.

"So, I'll see you tomorrow at the office?"

Matt gave him a pat on the shoulder once his jacket was back on. "You bet. Thanks for the beer."

"You're just like my own kid, Matt. Remember I'm just looking out for you." Derek gave him a long look before opening the door and heading out into the rain.

Matt shut it and cursed. What the hell was that all about? Since when was his life this complicated? It was getting harder and harder to ignore this supposed history Derek had with Kate.

He walked back to the kitchen. He needed food. He reached for his phone on the counter and dialed the pizza place number from memory. It was that kind of night. Maybe he'd eat in front of his laptop and get some paperwork done. There were cases that needed reviewing. Then maybe he could stop thinking about Kate. Describing Kate as "hard to get" was putting it mildly, but he knew she wasn't playing games. She was seriously trying to take things slow.

He pushed himself off the counter, satisfied that food would be arriving in under an hour, and grabbed a beer. He looked out into the almost dark ravine behind his house. This was a place he was grateful for every day and it was a site he never got tired of. He had made all of this himself and for a long time he'd been certain he wanted to share his life with someone, start a family. But then shit had happened, his career had consumed him, changed him, until finally when the accident had happened, his relationship with Michelle had been destroyed. It was only after months of blaming himself that he realized she hadn't been the right woman for him.

He had always wanted a chance to build the family life he would have loved to have as a child. Michelle had just been the wrong woman. He had held so much back from her. He never talked or shared anything about himself. He hadn't been compelled to, not the way he was with Kate. He wanted to know everything about her, and he didn't mind talking about himself. He also liked being silent with her, as cheesy as it sounded, and it wasn't anything he'd ever admit out loud. He just liked being with her.

But there was something off, and it was so damned tempting to take Liam up on his offer to do some digging on her. On Derek. What was this connection they had? Hell, he'd just blown off the man he thought of as a father because of Kate. What was that saying? Did he doubt Derek? Or did he want to believe Kate at all costs? Was his judgment already being clouded?

He braced his hands on the counter and stretched his

bad leg, exhaling raggedly at the stab of pain. The doorbell sounded. It was too early for the pizza. He forced himself to swallow the pain and walked to the entry.

He opened the door to find Kate standing there under a red umbrella, holding a cardboard tray with two Starbucks cups, and a hesitant, but gorgeous smile on her face. "You're the nicest view I've seen all day," he said. He'd missed her. He took the tray from her hands so she could close her umbrella and held the door for her to walk in.

"I heard you weren't at work."

"My sister," he said, taking her coat and hanging it up on a hook on the closet door.

She nodded.

"I thought you couldn't deal with seeing me until Thanksgiving," he said, taking a step closer to her, catching the scent of citrus and coffee.

She smiled up at him. "You and the turkey were battling for first in my mind." He was laughing as he bent his head to kiss her. He loved that she met him halfway. He backed Kate up against the closet, all the while keeping their lips together. He had missed her more than he realized. She wrapped her arms around him, and he placed his hands on her hips and stood between her legs. Kate kissed him back, like she missed him just as much. The doorbell rang.

"Who's that?" she mumbled against him. He liked the fact that she hadn't let go of him.

"Dinner," he said, pushing himself away. He fumbled around in his pocket for some cash and then answered the door. "Hey, Pete," he said, handing him the right change.

"Hi, Matt. Got your usual. Have a good night."

"You too, buddy."

He shut the door and turned to look at Kate. For some reason she was smiling, a little smugly. "That looks like feeling-sorry-for-yourself food."

"I never feel sorry for myself."

"Uh-huh," she said with a cute little smirk. She picked up the box of tiramisu and raised an eyebrow. "I know an emotional binge when I see one."

"I like dessert, and this looks like a woman who's hungry, but doesn't want to admit that she wants to inhale half this food right along with me," he said, smacking a kiss on her open mouth and walking into the family room. He was trying his damnedest not to limp or cringe as he stepped down into the sunken room. He heard her picking up the coffee and walking after him, laughing. He flicked on the gas fireplace switch and turned to her.

"So, you're staying for dinner?"

"I can't let you gorge yourself in this pitiful state."

He grinned as he set the food on the coffee table. "You're just hungry and using me for dinner, not that I'm complaining." They divvied up some pizza slices and settled onto the couch. When most of the pizza was inhaled, she leaned over and handed him a coffee.

"That was really great bad pizza," she said, taking a sip of her coffee.

"Giusseppe's has provided many a meal for me," he said. "So where's Janie tonight?"

"She's at home. I called her on the way over. Cara is working with them on a family tree project due next week." She toyed with the lid of her coffee cup.

He took a sip of the semi-warm coffee. "Do you, uh, have much history to go on for that?"

She shook her head, meeting his gaze. "Not really, so we decided we'd make it fun and mention all of us and focus on the different types of families there are out there. None of us are actually related, Matt."

He didn't move for a moment, holding her stare. His conversation with Derek came back to him and he had the urge to ask her, except she had come here of her own volition, and he knew that was a big deal for her. He'd be risking her walking right out if he pushed. He kept his features relaxed, his voice casual. "So Cara and Alex aren't your biological sisters?"

She shook her head, tucked a few strands of hair behind her ear, and took a sip of coffee. He cleared his throat after a minute. She finally glanced up at him. "We met at a foster home."

He leaned forward, resting his forearms on his thighs. "Where was your family?"

She opened her mouth and he read the insecurity in her expression, in the way her gaze darted from his. She swallowed a few times and he knew the rapid beating of his heart was because he was anticipating the truth, whatever it was, would not be easy to hear, but would reveal a hell of a lot about her. "My mom died when I was fifteen."

"I'm sorry." He didn't move, waiting for her to say something else.

She rubbed her hands on the front of her jeans and he reached over, placing his hand on the nape of her neck. He couldn't sit here and not touch her when he'd never witnessed a woman so desperately in need of being held. He forgot the warnings from Derek. He forgot everything except the feeling in his gut that made him want to give her whatever she needed. She raised her eyes to meet his stare. "It was a long time ago."

"Where was your father?"

"He died when I was six."

Her words were without emotion; the only hint he had that this was terrifying for her was the rapid rise and fall of her chest, like she was running. "You didn't have any other family you could have lived with?"

She shook her head and stood abruptly. His hand fell,

letting her leave. "So, now you know," she said with a shrug.

He'd lost her. He stood abruptly and then cursed under his breath as pain radiated through every inch of his leg and then ricocheted through his body. He squeezed his eyes shut for a moment.

"Are you okay? Let me get you something."

He kept his teeth clenched together and tried to focus as the pain lessened to a dull throb. "I'm okay," he whispered hoarsely. He hated this. They weren't supposed to be talking about him right now. "I want to finish our conversation."

"It is finished. And then I lived happily ever after."

He forced a smile. He knew when to stop pushing. "Cute."

Her eyes were filled with concern and she put her coffee down. "You aren't taking anything for pain, are you? You need some ibuprofen at least."

"Not much of a fan."

"That's ridiculous. At least take something to take the edge off."

"You could help me take the edge off," he said, unable to hide his grin as her eyes narrowed on him, hands on her nicely-shaped hips. He liked the jeans, and the woman in the jeans.

"See, the first was ridiculous. The second is just wishful thinking," she said with an adorable smirk as she left the room. This woman was killing him. She was here because she obviously cared about him, but she was still at arm's length. She had opened up, though, even if it wasn't much. It meant she trusted him. Derek's warning played back and he shrugged it off. Whatever was between them, he'd find out from Kate. He'd earn her trust and she'd let him in.

She walked back in a moment later and he told himself to keep his eyes on her. He let his gaze wander over her. She tossed her purse on the couch before grabbing her ringing phone from the inside. "I have Advil somewhere in there," she whispered as she answered the call.

"I don't rifle through women's purses looking for period medication."

She chucked it onto his lap. "Don't be a pubescent Neanderthal," she whispered. "Huh, no, sorry, Cara I wasn't speaking to you. Yup…"

He tuned out of her conversation and grudgingly looked for the bottle of Advil. He decided he'd rather pop a pill for a chance at a somewhat decent evening than stay in pain and risk her leaving. His hands circled around a small pill bottle and he pulled it out. Not Advil. It was a prescription drug for anxiety. He knew because his mother had the exact same prescription.

He looked up at Kate just as she ended the call. Her eyes locked onto his. Her skin turned a shade of white that he hadn't seen before. He didn't say a thing, waiting.

She quickly reached out and he opened his hand for her, letting her grab the bottle. "That's nothing," she whispered and his stomach clenched as the sound of humiliation strangled the lighthearted mood.

He struggled to find the right words, the ones that would make her want to explain. "You don't have to be embarrassed."

She grabbed her purse, swung it over her shoulder, and stood. "I'm not."

He stood and cursed, his stupid leg feeling like it was filled with shards of glass. He was able to grab her wrist before she totally walked out of his life. "Don't be mad at me."

"I'm not," she said, looking somewhere over his shoulder.

"But you're about to walk out of here because…"

She frowned and then shrugged, looking so much less defensive, so much less the tough girl he'd nicknamed her. "I'm a private person and that was something private."

He tugged her gently over to him, an inch or so from his

body. "Have I ever pressured you for anything? Even when you told me you lived happily ever after, I accepted that crappy exit. I know there's a helluva lot more."

She shook her head and didn't say anything for a long moment. "I keep the bottle in my bag as insurance. It's a safety net. I haven't had to take one in over five years."

His heart pounded relentlessly. The PI in him wanted all the details. He was becoming more and more intrigued by and concerned about her history. The guy in him that cared more about her than he ever would have expected this early on felt bad for her, for the vulnerability that was etched in the dip of her gorgeous mouth, in the softness of her voice. "Why did you start taking them?"

She crossed her arms under her breasts and, for the first time since he met her, the sudden appearance of cleavage didn't really register. He just wanted to know she was okay. She looked down at her feet. "I had some issues in my childhood, things that happened to me...and sometimes I'd hear a sound or be in a situation that would trigger a memory and then all of a sudden I wouldn't be able to breathe and I'd hate the feel of my own skin. I'd want to disappear, but I couldn't get away from myself. It was an awful feeling."

"Was it your mom dying that caused the anxiety?"

She drew a deep breath. "Other stuff."

Other stuff. That was all he was getting tonight. "What made you get past that?"

"Being with Alex and Cara again, having a real home. Feeling safe. Janie. It was like everything started coming together for me," she said softly, her eyes watering for a moment.

He rubbed the back of his neck. "I'm glad everything worked out." What a stupid thing to say, but being with her was like walking the finest damn line, a step in the wrong direction and he'd be gone.

"I should probably get going. It's a school night and I've got grading to do, and then we're going to look over some real estate listings for the group home." She took a step back from him, walls up and her posture stiff.

"Why does it feel like every time we get close you shut down? You're running off. Just a few minutes ago you had the whole night. Now—"

"I'm not. This is life with kids and a job and a fundraiser."

"No, it's you not wanting to share everything."

"I just shared a bunch. Mother died when I was young. Went to foster care. Anxiety. There."

"How about what happened that caused the anxiety?"

"There are things I don't share with anyone."

He took a step into her, hating that she visibly stiffened. "I'm not anyone, not anymore, as much as you want to deny it. I know you better than you think, just like you know me. There's no denying this thing between us."

"If I don't deny it then you become real in a way that terrifies the crap out of me, Matt. I spent my entire life believing guys like you didn't exist, and I'm so afraid that if I believe in you, you'll fail me. If I don't believe in you, then I can't get hurt."

"If you think I'll fail you, then what are you doing here?"

"I don't know," she whispered. "I can't stay away."

That was all he needed to hear before trying to convince her without words that he was the real thing. For her, he could be anything she wanted.

Chapter Nine

It smelled like a little bit of heaven inside their house.

Kate jogged down the stairs, ready to tackle the coats and boots at the front entryway. Matt, his mother, and his sister would be arriving in less than half an hour, and she was nervous, which was kind of silly. A part of her really wanted to meet his mother, but it also implied seriousness about what they were. Once you met family...it became harder to walk away, but she'd be an absolute idiot to walk away from the man who somehow succeeded at breaking down almost all of her walls, who made it abundantly clear he wanted her and her daughter. And, like every other time she thought about that night at the fair, when he'd looked at her, his gorgeous eyes filled with unmistakable tenderness and sincerity, and he'd told her it was okay to be soft, she melted. He was unlike anyone she'd ever met.

When she'd filled Alex and Cara in on most of the evening's events, Alex insisted she invite Matt's family here. Since she knew Alex was a total control freak when it came to the holiday and the cooking, she had. He'd replied minutes later. No games, no waiting. He accepted.

She lined up what seemed like a dozen shoes outside the closet, hung their jackets, and made some room inside the closet.

"I've been kicked out of the kitchen already," Cara said, holding an armful of toys as she walked toward her.

"I'm not even going in there," Kate said, closing the closet doors. Alex loved to take over holiday cooking, and since she and Cara loathed cooking, they had happily agreed to let her. They were relegated to such tasks as cleaning up the house, setting the table, and getting flowers.

"Seriously, where does all this crap come from?" Cara dumped the toys into a giant basket and set it on the stairs, ready to go up to the girls' room. She turned to Kate. "So, you nervous about meeting Matt's mother?"

"It's not like that." Kate looked in the mirror and smoothed her hair. How it had gone from nicely styled to disheveled in less than an hour was beyond her.

Cara narrowed her eyes and crossed her arms. "Really?"

"Yes. It was more like you guys bullied me to invite them, so I did. Not a big deal, almost accidental."

"Sure. It's about as accidental as that new lip gloss you're wearing."

Kate smacked her lips together.

"Seriously, you don't have to hide from me. You are obviously falling for this guy and there's no point in denying it." Cara's features softened and she sat down on the stair landing. "I know it must be scary for you, opening up to a guy, and I know how bad you had it. But there are good ones out there, and it's okay to trust the good ones. I have a feeling about him, Kate."

Kate crossed her arms. Everything her sister was saying was true. She knew it, deep down, with Matt. She had learned to fine-tune her instincts early in life; she could analyze mannerisms, expressions, and tone of voice. She knew he wasn't putting on an act. She felt it when he reached for her, when he kissed her, when he looked at her. He was one of the good guys. Maybe that's what made it so difficult because, if she didn't want to lose him, she was going to have to open up to him eventually. He was going to demand more of her than she had ever given someone.

The doorbell jarred both of them. Cara snatched up the basket and started up the stairs. "I'll be down in a second. Go make a good impression with 'the mom.'"

Kate took a deep breath and swung open the door. Of course, her eyes went to Matt first, because that seemed to be what always happened. He was a good foot taller than his mother and sister, who were standing in front of him.

"Happy Thanksgiving," Sabrina said and they all began speaking at once, exchanging pleasantries, as Kate led them inside.

Matt laid a quick, but very real, kiss on her lips, before taking his mother's and sister's coats.

"It's so wonderful to meet you, Kate. Thank you for inviting us to your lovely home," his mother said warmly. She had dark hair like Matt, cut into a stylish bob, and she was petite. She wore a deep-red sweaterdress and was holding a large dish, which Kate took from her when she held it out.

"It's great to meet you as well, Ms. Lane," Kate said, feeling more at ease than she would have expected so quickly.

"Call me Barb," she said with a smile.

Loud, fast footsteps and riotous laughter filled the hallway as all three girls tore into the area, followed by Alex and Cara. Kate didn't know what Matt had said about Janie or how he had explained why they were all living together, but when Kate made the introductions, Matt's mother didn't blink an eye as she shook Janie's hand. If anything, her expression warmed even more.

"Alex, it smells amazing in here," Matt said, leaning down so Janie could climb onto his back. When this unspoken piggyback situation had started, she had no idea, but her daughter's arms were around Matt's neck, and she looked... like she'd never, ever been happier.

"Thanks, everything should be ready in about an hour."

"I brought some pumpkin pie," Barb said.

"Oh that's lovely, thank you," Alex said, pushing her hair off her face.

"Now, put us to work. I like to feel busy," Barb said, following Alex as she led them into the kitchen.

"Just don't let Matt near the food. He samples everything without asking," Sabrina said.

"Nice," he said, nudging her shoulder. Janie laughed at the jostling movement. "But also true. Why don't I keep the kids entertained?"

The girls were already jumping up and down.

"That's perfect. Matt thinks just like a kid," Sabrina said with a big grin.

"You can help me. You're about the same size as them."

He winked at Kate and then was walking down the hallway toward the family room, Cassandra and Beth leading the way, Janie attached to his back like he did this every day. Like he belonged here.

Half an hour later, the table was almost set, Alex was bustling around the kitchen in her "zone" while Barb had made herself at home and was chopping cucumbers and tomatoes for the salad. Kate was reaching for the stack of dessert plates when Barb stopped chopping and gave her a look that was startlingly similar to Matt's.

"Kate, I just wanted to let you know that I think what you're doing is very special, adopting Janie," she said in a soft voice.

Kate tensed for a second before setting the dishes on the

counter. She didn't know how much Matt had told his mother. Considering how little she'd told him, Barb was probably guessing what her situation was. "Thank you, but I'm not special. I mean, adopting Janie shouldn't be a special thing, you know?"

Barb smiled and looked beyond her, toward the open family room where Matt was currently, and very loudly, winning a round of the *Frozen* memory game. "You're absolutely right, but I do know you're probably being modest. A young woman with a busy career, no husband, adopting a child? It's impressive. And wonderful. I also know you're very good for my son."

Kate turned slightly and smiled at the picture he made with the girls and his sister. Janie was sitting in his lap. "He's a good man," she said, glad to be saying it out loud. She knew where Matt got his easy demeanor and good nature. His mother was warm and welcoming, assuming only the best in her.

"He is a good man. I don't know if everything would have turned out the same if he hadn't been so strong. I regret every day that I stayed with their father as long as I did, but I can't go back and change that. It forced Matt to grow up much faster than he should have had to. And I'm aware every day of the sacrifices my son made for his sister and me. He deserves a good woman," she said, patting Kate's hand.

Barb glanced away for a moment, and then started speaking again, tossing the cucumbers into the wooden serving bowl. "I'm not sure how much he's told you about what happened to him after the accident...and I do hate to interfere in his life," she said, placing the wooden serving spoons in the bowl and lowering her voice.

Kate leaned in closer, very experienced in the subtleties of girl-talk, living in a house full of women.

"It was the only time I've seen him down. He loved

working on the force, which didn't exactly make it easy for a mother to sleep at night, but I knew he loved his work. I'll never forget when his wife called me in the middle of the night to tell me he'd been shot and was in the OR, not knowing if he was going to make it or not. That's not a call a mother ever wants to get. But, as I'm sure you know, Matthew is a fighter. Even when they told him he might not be able to use that leg again, he pulled through. His marriage slowly fell apart during his recovery. I know he blamed himself, saying that he was miserable to be around, but I always knew she wasn't right for him."

Kate clutched the chair with her sweating palms. Her heart broke for Matt because, even though he'd told her the bare bones version of this story, he'd left out the details that made it real. And of course he would, because he never let on that there was a vulnerable side to him. He was the protector—for his mother, his sister—and he'd inadvertently started filling that role in her and Janie's life. But what his mother was saying about his ex...the way she said it implied that she knew his ex wasn't right for him, but that she was.

"I'm glad he's better," Kate said, reaching for the plates. She was lame. The woman was opening up to her, and all she could say was that she was glad he was better? *C'mon, Kate. Open up. Say something else.*

Barb gave her a knowing look before picking up the spoons and tossing the salad.

"I mean, I'm enjoying getting to know him, but I'm not in a position to jump into relationships. I'm committed to providing a good home to Janie and I don't want anything upsetting that."

"You're a lot wiser than I was at your age, sweetie, and I know you don't want me going on about how wonderful my son is..." She looked up at her, winked, and then said, "but he is."

Kate laughed.

"Dinner's ready!" Alex called, opening the oven door. The kitchen was suddenly awash with the smell of turkey, the richness of wine, and Matt as he suddenly appeared behind Kate. She felt her body welcome him, aware of the way her body leaned back into him. His arms reached around her to snatch a cucumber from the bowl. His mother swatted his hand with the spoon, picked up the bowl, and walked to the dining room.

Matt leaned into her, his lips brushing against her ear. "Somehow, I'm going to get you alone after."

• • •

Three hours later, after one of the best meals he'd ever eaten, Matt was itching to get Kate to himself. Sensing an opportunity when Alex declared that she was brewing coffee and getting dessert set up while his mother and the rest of them started clearing the table, he made eye contact with Kate and tilted his head toward the back door.

A slight smile teased her lips, and he was suddenly hungry all over again. For her. Today had been an exercise in severe self-control. He hadn't felt like sharing. He barely felt that he'd had enough time with Kate on his own, let alone having to share her with his nosy sister and his ever-optimistic mother. He knew she approved of Kate. She kept engaging her in conversation, and even when Kate politely, but obviously, turned the conversation away from herself, his mother seemed to still like her. A hundred bucks said his mother and sister had come up with some reason that Kate was closed-off, or maybe they assumed she was shy.

Whatever it was, and however much he wanted Kate to himself, he had to admit it'd been a good day. He liked her sisters, and the girls...Janie...he liked spending time with them. He stood against the brick wall, on the deck, away from the windows and waited for Kate. Sure enough, a minute later she walked outside, wrapping her arms around herself against the chilly October wind. Every time he saw her, he wanted her more. There were things he knew about people, about how they were on the inside, that made him sure about the way he felt for her. After the accident and his divorce, he had fine-tuned his people-reading skills, so he knew Kate was a no-bullshit, no-agenda type of woman. Even if she hadn't opened up to him, there was an inherent trust he had in her, which was beginning to make him question his friend. This morning he'd had to shrug off the guilt he felt at the idea that Derek was spending Thanksgiving by himself. What was Derek's problem with her? Even more curious, how the hell did they even know each other?

"I need you to tell me something," he said, pulling her hair from her face as the wind tossed it around. She was standing in front of him and her typical, slightly defensive look was gone; he hadn't seen it in a week at least. Progress, until now.

Her lips narrowed slightly. He knew she had her secrets, he knew she wasn't ready to give them all up. That was fine. He'd ask about Derek when the time was right. He was after one answer though. "Who's Art?"

She frowned, obviously pretending to be confused. "Who?"

"That other guy you had a date with, Art Zibbits."

This time he frowned as she burst out laughing. He wasn't the jealous type, but he also didn't like the idea of another man in her life. Not now, not when she meant so much to him. Kate was clutching the front of his sweater, taking huge gasping breaths. It might have been funny if they weren't talking about another man.

"Uh, hello? Zibbits?"

She shook her head, smile still there, laughter still threatening. "*You* are Art Zibbits."

She drummed her fingers along his chest, and he had to clench his teeth in order to stay focused on what she was saying. "That night you walked into the bar? Alex and Cara were trying to convince me to pick up some random guy... and when you walked in you were the one."

He liked where this was going.

"And since we make code names for everyone so the girls won't be able to follow adult conversation, you were officially given the code name Art Exhibit."

He didn't hold back his smile. He leaned down for a kiss and was stopped by her hand on his chest.

"I realize this may inflate your already slightly-exploding male ego."

He was laughing when he kissed her again.

"Come home with me tonight," he whispered against her lips. Her body stiffened against him, and she pulled back slightly. He loosened his grip on her, not wanting her to feel trapped. Her reaction wasn't exactly the one he was hoping for. He searched her eyes. The fear he saw gutted him. He schooled his features so as to not let on that he knew she was afraid. Of him, of intimacy, of spending the night? He had no idea.

She stared at his shoulder for a second then met his gaze. "It's Thanksgiving and—"

"Later. Tonight. I'll pick you up. I'll drive my mother and sister home then I can pick you up after the girls are asleep."

She still didn't say anything, but she didn't pull away. Her hands were on the front of his chest. He didn't know if she kept them there because she liked touching him, or if she liked that she'd be able to push him away easily. He took the opportunity to convince her without words. He leaned forward, sank his hands into her hair at the nape of her neck, and pulled her in gently. His mouth kissed the sweet, soft spot beneath her ear and he drank in the smell of her—cinnamon and vanilla and Kate. He kissed a slow trail until he reached her lips, where she was waiting for him. Her hands wrapped around his neck and she pressed against him, kissing him back with the same pent-up need.

"How am I supposed to say no to you?" she whispered, pulling her mouth away slightly. He wasn't ready to let her go yet, so he kissed her again. And again.

"Then don't," he said against her lips.

"Omigod, Matt. Seriously? Groping my teacher on Thanksgiving? I was supposed to come out here and tell you dessert is ready, but it looks like you've already helped yourself."

Kate laughed softly. She was about to pull away, but Matt held her hips to his. "Don't move."

"Omigod," his sister mumbled again, slamming the door. Not before he heard her grumbling about deserving bonus marks due to trauma.

"Your family is just as nosy as mine," Kate said, pulling away.

Matt rolled his shoulders. "Yeah. So, tonight. I'll pick you up at nine?"

She nodded, her expression somewhere between wary and heated.

• • •

"I think I'm going to explode."

Cara threw a pillow at Alex, who was currently sprawled across Kate's bed, with the top button of her jeans undone. "Well, maybe you should stop cooking like Paula Deen and we'd all have a chance of not bursting through our jeans."

Kate wasn't paying attention to them. She was currently

trying not to panic, but she was panicking. Big time. If she were still taking anxiety meds, she probably would have had to take one, but she hadn't needed to in five years. She wasn't going back. But she was also going to have to dig deep into her breathing and visualization techniques to make it through.

"Why are you darting around the room like a squirrel on uppers?" Alex asked.

Kate stopped moving, halfway between her closet and dresser. She *was* darting around. "I don't know."

"Is it because Matt is coming over?"

That was the other thing—she hadn't told them that she was spending the night at his house. Really, she was acting like a teenager planning on sneaking out of her room after her parents went to sleep. She had come so far, yet it was moments like these that reminded her of how far she still had to go. Miles. And more freaking miles.

"Right, and I'm going to spend the night at his place."

"It's about time, really."

"Exactly what I was thinking. If Matt were my boyfriend I would've jumped him the first night," Alex said, flopping back on the bed. Cara snorted her agreement.

Kate stopped in front of her closet and raised an eyebrow. "Right."

Alex nodded, crossing her bunny-slipper feet at the ankle. "Yep, except I'd probably knock the man over with all my extra, puff-pastry-induced weight. But that man...not an ounce of puffiness. And seriously, the way he was with the girls? You know he's a keeper, right? Like we don't have to convince you of that too, do we?"

Kate rolled her eyes. She couldn't get serious with them tonight. They were breaking down all her last walls. Like Matt hadn't already done a fine job. "Yes, he's great with kids."

"And Janie. He adores her," Cara said. "You know you

can trust him, with everything."

Kate flopped onto the edge of the bed. "I haven't told him, if that's what you're hinting at."

"Anything?"

She shrugged and then fell back, staring at the ceiling. "I told him my mother died, I met you two in foster care, and that's about it."

She could see from the corner of her eye that they were looking back and forth and mouthing things silently. She wondered who would speak first.

"It isn't random that you ran into Matt at the bar, then at school," Cara said. "What are the odds? Maybe he came into your life because he is the one. I remember that feeling, knowing someone instantly."

"What you and Jack had was entirely different. You guys were teenagers and on the street."

"No one has ever come close to him again," Cara whispered. Kate squeezed her eyes shut. She hated how Cara's story ended. She hated knowing that Cara was secretly in love with someone from her past, someone she'd never see again.

"So, great. What you're saying is that Kate is meant to be with the hot ex-cop, you had the hots for a guy who is incomparable...where does that leave me? With the Pillsbury Doughboy?"

The pillow that was meant for Alex landed on Kate and she finally found the ability to laugh. It was the Doughboy image.

Cara stood with a start. "Enough of this. Watcha wearing tonight?"

That was the problem here. She knew exactly what they were going to do, and how could she forget? The second Matt had whispered in that raspy, deep, and—good God—hot voice, she knew she wouldn't be able to say no. But she also didn't want to look like she was about to go and jump the man. So, she should wear jeans and a sweater.

"Here, I've packed your bag, and I'm about to go through your underwear drawer and pick out something hot if you don't hurry up." Cara was dangling her small overnight bag in one hand while opening her lingerie drawer with the other. Kate slammed it shut.

"Seriously? You have no faith in me?"

"None whatsoever. You're looking for a way out of this."

"I was just thinking that if Janie wakes up during the night…"

"She never wakes up."

"But if she does, tell her that—"

"We'll tell her that you'll be back tomorrow and we're all home and she has nothing to worry about. I'll even sleep in her room if she needs me too."

"Okay, well if I hurry, I'll have time to tuck her in before I leave."

"Then stop talking and move."

She nodded, gathering her thoughts as she left the room. She had nothing to worry about. Janie was in the best hands. She needed to take a long shower and shave her legs. And then she needed to go and be a grown-up woman.

Kate tucked the covers under Janie's chin, loving the way she watched her. It was the look that little children gave their parents, the one babies gave their mothers, the look that said *you are my whole world*. That look filled up all her holes, her wounds, her empty places. Janie filled up all the places in her that were hardened and damaged. She made her believe in good and love.

"I liked Thanksgiving today," Janie said, taking off her

glasses.

Kate smiled, placing them on the nightstand.

Janie shook her head. "Put them on the unicorn."

Kate laughed. "What?"

Janie smiled. "So he can see at night."

It took a few tries to get the glasses to stay put, but eventually the pink unicorn was staring at them wisely.

Satisfied, Janie gave a nod.

"I'm glad. I had fun today too."

She pulled out her red ribbon from under the covers. "I'm going to sleep with my ribbon forever."

Kate tousled her soft brown hair. Janie was growing so fast and, despite all her fears about her daughter not being able to fit in, she was finding a place for herself. She was thriving. Janie wasn't the one with issues; she was. "Sure. I'm glad you had such a great time. "

She looked over at the giant unicorn that was staring at them beside the nightstand. Matt had surprised her. She knew he'd be nice to Janie; he had manners. He was a good guy. What he'd done for them at the restaurant, and at the fair went beyond good upbringing. He didn't have to defend Janie to the girls' parents at the restaurant. He didn't have to step in and get the unicorn. He didn't have to enter the race. But the look on his face when he realized what was going down when no one partnered with Janie had been…mesmerizing. He'd gotten this tough-ass, protective look that made her insides melt. Someone was defending them. Someone was defending Janie. And as much as she liked to believe she could do it all, it took a hell of a lot out of her. It was like she was constantly fighting. Her past and her present were blurring at times. Sometimes she felt like the little girl who'd been silenced with duct tape for calling out her stepfather, and she still couldn't get the tape off, couldn't speak. Sometimes she felt like a hero, who'd risen above it all and come out with this little princess.

"Matt is nice." Janie reached out for Kate's hand, tugging her down beside her. Kate stretched out on the bed and snuggled Janie, inhaling her sweet smell. She loved strawberry shampoo. Janie always smelled like strawberries and summer.

"He is," she said. Yeah, Matt was a lot of things. Guys like him didn't go to county fairs and try and win unicorns, or get royally pissed when a little girl they barely knew was excluded from a race. They didn't kiss like Matt did, like he wanted to thoroughly know her. Guys like that didn't make her feel safe. But he did.

"Cassy and Beth said that he's your boyfriend."

Janie was staring at her expectantly. Kate knew there was a disconnect, but she also knew she didn't want to underestimate what Janie was capable of understanding. "He is," she said with a nod.

"That's why he came here for Thanksgiving?""

Kate nodded.

"I like his mommy and sister."

Kate smiled. "They were really nice. I liked them too. And I liked the pumpkin pie his mom brought. I think I ate so much my pants are going to explode."

Janie burst out into a fit of uncontrollable giggles and Kate laughed along with her. "You're my snuggle monster," she said, giving her lots of kisses while Janie squealed with laughter. When they'd first met, Janie had been very quiet. She hadn't started speaking yet, walking was a struggle, and she was delayed in almost every major developmental milestone. Kate knew a lot of that was to be expected, but a lot of it was also because Janie needed extra attention, needed therapy. The home she had been placed in was decent, even if lacking the extra attention.

She'd connected with Janie the second she'd met her.

Janie's dark eyes were alert, and the smile she gave Kate had made her breath catch. Kate had stood there, immobile, in a strange internal place, somewhere between her past and her present. Janie had reminded her of her little sister. The way she smiled when Kate would enter the room, the light in her eyes. And then Janie did something that was so uniquely Janie that Kate was able to walk away from the past and get to know the little girl who would soon claim, heal, and capture her heart. Janie had laughed, a pure, loud, belly laugh that didn't sound like any other she'd ever heard. That day was the first day in a long adoption process that ended with Kate becoming a mother. And the six of them becoming a family.

Sometimes when she saw Alex and Cara, she'd get flashes of the three of them at that group home. Alex still laughed with the occasional snort that she refused to acknowledge. Cara still bossed them around. But they were her family and their little girls were her family. She'd never once thought she was lacking, until Matt came along. He had a killer smile, which was always somewhere between hot and mischievous. A stare that made her think he knew all about her, inside. And a body that...she wanted to explore, that she wanted to be close to. She wanted him to be real, all of it to be real and sure. For once, she was willing to let a man in. He'd won her over, but she knew this wouldn't be enough for him. Soon, he'd want more and she would have to decide how much she truly trusted him, how much of herself she could share.

"You're my mommy monster," Janie said, kissing her back. Kate snuggled in beside her and reached over to shut off the lamp. Right now, she just wanted to lie in this bed and hold the sweet girl who had given her more joy than she'd ever known until Janie fell asleep. And then she'd go with Matt.

• • •

Matt stood in the doorway, caught somewhere between being what he assumed was emotionally moved and scared. It was the picture of Janie and Kate, curled up together on the single bed. It was a picture of domestic bliss, of home, of warmth. It was something he'd always sought in the back of his mind, but nothing he'd ever actively tried for.

He ran his hands through his hair and stood like an oaf, struggling to find some direction. He knew the kind of man he wanted to be, the kind of husband he wanted to be. He'd screwed up the first time around. He knew at that point in his life he'd been searching for everything he never had growing up. He'd wanted to prove that he was capable of being a better man than his father and he had, though it didn't take much. But Michelle had been right about him, he had been emotionally closed off. It was the only way he'd been able to bury the shit in his childhood, and the only way to rationalize the shit he dealt with every day at his job. Until that asshole had shot him. He'd had no idea if he'd ever walk again. So yeah, he'd been closed off. Michelle had found what she needed in another guy's bed and their marriage imploded.

So standing here, in this house, with these women, should terrify him. Kate wasn't just a woman to go home with. She was a woman you built a home with. That should make him want to run. He still beat himself up over one failed marriage. Did he have what Kate and Janie needed? Right now, he'd say yes. He'd say anything to be part of the picture he saw in front of him. He wanted to lie on the bed with them, feel Kate's body against his, have Janie's hand curl around his. He wanted their trust. He wanted to keep them safe. He wanted to erase all the worry and secrets from Kate's gorgeous eyes.

He swallowed hard. Hell, he'd just answered his own question.

Janie opened her eyes and looked at him. She smiled and started waving. He grinned and quietly walked across the room, crouching down at her bedside. She pointed to the unicorn. Matt laughed softly at the glasses perched on the stuffed animal's nose.

"Nice look," he said. She slapped her hands across her mouth and giggled.

"Mommy's sleeping," she whispered, not-too-softly. "Her pants are 'sploding."

Matt laughed as Kate opened her eyes and groaned. "Janie, what are you saying?"

He and Janie laughed, even though he had no idea what was going on. She was pretty funny and Kate's face was red.

"You told me your pants were 'sploding," Janie said, gasping for air as she kept laughing.

Kate closed her eyes and shook her head. She leaned over, gave Janie a kiss and stood up. "I think I may have mentioned something about eating too much today."

Janie looked back and forth between them and he felt something, like a flash of how things could be with them. "Night, Matt," Janie whispered. She looked up at him with the unmistakable sheen of admiration in her eyes, so much so that his stomach clenched. He leaned down and kissed her forehead.

He smiled when Kate looked over at him. She tucked the covers around Janie and gave her a kiss.

"Good night, sweetie."

"Night mommy." They walked out of the room quietly and Kate shut the door behind her, on the picture of the life he wanted. She walked straight into his arms.

And he knew there was no walking away from these two.

Chapter Ten

Matt handed Kate a glass of wine and wanted to curse at the formality of this. He knew there were secrets, but he felt like he was walking on eggshells around her. She took the glass, gave him a small smile, and then looked out the window. It was pitch black outside. They were standing in the great room adjacent the kitchen, and she was staring through the large windows as though she could actually make something out. There was no one out there.

He'd half expected her not to come here tonight, giving an excuse. So despite the fact that she was holding a helluva lot inside, she did trust him, and that made up for it. She was wearing her kick-ass boots tonight, with dark jeans and a pale pink, soft-looking sweater. She looked gorgeous. Her hair was down and every part of him was dying to be with her.

He walked over to where she was, standing behind her, making eye contact in their reflection. He wanted to watch her, he wanted to see his hands on her, see the desire that lit her face as he touched her, but he didn't, because he felt her tense when he stood an inch from her body. She was one woman he couldn't figure out. He'd figured his ex out. All the other women he'd been with had been easy to read, and the second they'd wanted more, he was gone. For the first time, he was at a complete loss with the one woman who mattered.

"You all right?" he asked, jamming one fisted hand into his jeans pocket, the other tightening around the wine glass. He needed to keep his hands occupied.

She nodded, took a sip of wine, and shook her head. "I came here tonight because I want to be with you, but there are a few things you need to know about me."

"This isn't where you tell me you're actually a guy, is it?"

There was the tiniest hint of a smile for a second. She looked down into her glass and then up at his reflection again. "This is where I tell you I'm a sham."

He didn't say a thing as she turned around to look at him. "What are you talking about?"

"I stand up in front of a room full of teenagers and I talk like I know things. I know shit, Matt."

She was going down in his book as the most complex woman he'd ever known. She spoke in riddles. A thousand thoughts were going through him. Did she somehow fake her degree? Lie on her résumé? Did this have something to do with what Derek had warned him about?

"I project this image of a woman who's got it all together. Wise. Successful. Strong."

"That's accurate."

"What if I told you that something happened in my past, and I'm not ready to tell you about it, that has impacted every single decision I've made and it's prevented me from getting close to a man?"

"Do you want to tell me what happened?"

She shook her head.

"I told you all my dark, dirty secrets," he said, attempting humor.

"This goes beyond…this is stuff I've only ever shared with Alex and Cara. You know when something so bad happens that all you see is black? That just the thought of it weighs you down until you can't move? It pulls you under, and you can't easily get back out?"

He wrapped his arms around her, maybe as much for himself as for her. He expected her to shove him away, but she didn't. She clutched the sides of his shirt and buried her face in the hollow of his neck. He kissed the top of her head and brushed his lips against her ear. "You don't have to tell me, not now, but I know enough about you and me to know that we aren't just a fling. You've trusted me up until now."

She turned her face up to his, her lips reaching for him. He cupped her face gently with his hands and proceeded to kiss her thoroughly, deeply, until neither of them had the desire to speak. The emotions she evoked in him were like nothing he'd ever experienced. The first night he'd met her at the bar he'd wanted to go to bed with her. He'd had an insane attraction to her, found her gorgeous and drop-dead sexy, and now he wanted her even more, was even more attracted. Except now he also wanted to wake up with her, wanted to know every part of her.

Matt kissed her until she couldn't stand on her own. Her knees wobbled. He picked her up, sat her on the counter, and stood between her legs. Everything became hotter, fast. Their hands bumped into each other, competing for access, and he let her win as she pulled his shirt off. He lifted her and walked with her legs wrapped around his waist into his bedroom.

"You're not carrying me." He didn't feel like pointing out that she made no attempt to disengage herself.

"I *am*, because I don't want you to let go."

"Well, it's not very smart, because of your leg injury."

"Sex rule number one? Don't remind a guy about any inadequacies."

She laughed softly and leaned forward to kiss his neck. "We both know your ego isn't that fragile. Maybe you should use a cane."

He dropped her on the bed, both of them laughing. He followed her down only to have her wrestle him underneath her. She straddled him, out of breath. When he made eye contact with her, the humor was gone, something changing in her expression. His room was dark, but the faint glow of light from the hallway streamed through, enough that he could make out every expression, every flicker in her eyes.

She leaned down, took his hands off her waist, and placed them beside his head. She didn't break his stare. There was a look in her eyes, something other than desire. The room was quiet except for the sound of their breathing. He waited, knowing she needed to make the next move, knowing this wasn't going to be like anything he'd ever experienced. God, he'd wait forever, even if it killed him. She sat there, on top of him, and he sensed he was being evaluated, tried for some crime he had or hadn't committed.

He tried to figure her out, as he'd done countless times before, studying her unreadable expression. After another minute he slowly lowered his hands to grasp her thighs, feeling the heat through the soft denim. He didn't say a word as he grasped the edge of her sweater and she lowered her head as he lifted it off and tossed it to the floor. His gaze roamed over her bared torso appreciatively, taking in the full breasts, the black lace bra. With self-control he hadn't known he possessed, he kept his hands on her waist, her soft, pale skin a contrast to his. Her eyes were still on him, like she was expecting something. He knew her guard hadn't come down yet. He didn't have her trust yet. And he knew she wasn't waiting for words. Whatever darkness Kate had, whatever wounds, he knew they wouldn't be healed by some compliments. He knew that what she needed from him wasn't words.

"Matt," she whispered.

Hell, there was only so much he could stand. Kate, straddling him, in his bed, with only a bra on was heaven and hell. He'd never been one to linger. Her breath caught slightly as he grazed the underside of her breasts, his gaze not leaving hers. Her thighs squeezed him and she pressed against him, slowly leaning down to kiss him. He fisted his hands in her hair gently and kissed her until their breathing was ragged, until they both needed so much more.

. . .

Kate stared at the gorgeous, sleeping man she was lying half on top of. She stared at him and wondered if he was actually real. There wasn't a fake thing about him. He was as real as the smattering of scars across his beautiful, lean-muscled body. As real as all the wonderful, exquisite things they'd done in bed. She fought the urge to kiss him, or trace her finger over his lips. He looked peaceful, calm, and at the same time, he looked strong and capable and protective. His hand lay against her bare hip, keeping her close, safe. The even sound of his breathing was the only sound other than the flickering fire.

He'd known. He'd known he was her first and that would mean questions. She didn't want questions. This is what she'd always been afraid of, but there had never been anyone before him that she'd wanted enough to face those questions. She almost felt like she could, with Matt.

"I know you're watching me." She jumped at the sound of his voice. His eyes were still closed, but he was smiling now.

She leaned forward and kissed him, smiling. Seconds later she was still smiling, except he'd rolled her onto her back and she was staring up at him.

"So, have I proven myself?"

She laughed softly as he leaned forward, kissing her neck. The laughing turned into a sigh as he nuzzled her ear, kissing the spot beneath her earlobe. "I think so. Zibbits has nothing on you."

"Cute."

She ran her hands up the taught muscles of his biceps. "Best night ever," she whispered, marveling at how easy it was to be truthful with him.

He looked up, his eyes darkening before kissing her in that way that always seemed to capture all her thoughts, render her completely incapable of thinking of anything but him. "I want everything, all of you," he whispered gruffly. "I want you to let me in."

"I believe I just let you in," she said, attempting humor, but his expression turned serious and the conversation that she had always known would be demanded of her one day was imminent. She glanced at his shoulder and wanted to reach up and kiss it, knowing his flesh would be warm, strong.

"Kate? No more hiding. We're in a real relationship. I'm not walking away, I'm not playing games."

"Then what about you? I know your mother told me you were shot...and I know about Michelle. But nothing more." His face tensed slightly. She knew that by asking him, she was opening herself up to more questions.

"Okay. When I was a rookie cop, I got called out on a domestic call. It wasn't a new one. I had been to this apartment a few times. Every time, the wife would change her mind and not press charges. Her husband was a miserable drunk and would always lay into her when he got home from the bar. I wasn't surprised when I got the call that night. I walked in there, everything looking like it usually did—except this time, the wife said she was leaving and she was pressing charges. Her asshole husband was livid and said she couldn't take the kids. Everything was fine. Under control. Except the two-year-old came up to me, lifting her arms for me to pick her up. And uh," he blinked a few times, turning from her and looking up at the ceiling. She held her breath, waiting for him to finish. "I was thrown off for a second. I lost sight of what I was doing there and I took my eyes off the husband. I just looked down at that little girl and saw my sister. She used to do that too when my dad was on a bender. But that fucker pulled out a gun and shot his wife. I threw myself in front of her, shielded the kid, but by the time I drew my firearm he'd already shot me in the hip."

"Oh, Matt," she whispered, kissing his shoulder, holding on to him. She thought he'd pull away from her, but instead, he turned into her, kissed her.

"What happened?"

"The mother was okay. She got custody of the kids and he went to prison."

"What about you?"

He shrugged. "Never got full use of my leg back in a way that would be safe for me to work as a cop. It was stupid and I regret ever letting my past cloud my judgment. I was trained to compartmentalize. I had been able to do it before. But that one night, that one extra second...I, uh, was never able to talk about it with Michelle."

He stopped abruptly. The significance of what he was saying filled her with emotion. "Why?"

"I don't know. We never had that kind of relationship. We went through the motions. I thought that's what love was. She didn't share and I didn't share. I didn't lean on her or confide in her. I didn't know that I needed that kind of involvement with someone. She found it with someone else, while we were married. Next time around, I want someone who can give me everything, because that's what I'm willing do to."

She held her breath. The weight of this burden he had suddenly thrust upon her made it hard to breathe. "Matt," she whispered, reading the expectation in his eyes.

"Hey, you can't just walk away from everything. We've come way too far, baby. I've shared everything about myself. Everything. I know more about you than you'd like to think." He gripped her hips gently, holding her still. "I know you, Kate. I know what turns you on, I know all the little sounds you make when I'm inside you, and I know there hasn't been a guy before me."

Her gaze snapped to his, but she had no words.

"Why hasn't there been anyone?"

"I never should have dated a PI."

"It didn't take a detective."

"I'm not even going to ask how you knew."

"I can tell you in explicit detail if needed—"

"Not needed."

"Kate?"

"I haven't needed relationships other than my sisters and our kids. I have spent most of my life surviving, and I quickly realized that when there wasn't a man in my life, I thrived."

There was a long pause. Her mind was trying to sort through everything he'd told her, everything he was demanding of her. But she couldn't come up with a way out or a way to stay with him.

He took her hand, and she just watched as he kissed the palm of her hand. "So it must have been really bad, at home? To go your whole life without having a relationship."

She avoided eye contact with him, because the man just kept on reeling her in. "There's more to life than sex. Survival takes priority. A job. Adopting Janie. I could not afford to let my guard down for a guy. Not worth it until—" She stopped speaking, but she knew they both knew what she'd been about to say. Until him. The risk had never been worth it. She had never trusted anyone like she trusted him. Until now, until Matt.

"Thank you," he said, kissing her shoulder. "I need to ask you something. Can you tell me who Derek Stinson is to you?"

She gasped. "Pardon?"

"Derek Stinson. How do you know him?"

And just like that, Derek found his way back into her life, ruining it. She stopped breathing for a moment. She was trapped. That monster. It *had* been him at the bar. And now... She pulled back. She wanted him, wanted to stay the way they were before Derek was involved, but she couldn't go back. Moving forward with him now would jeopardize her safety, her family, everything if he believed Derek over her.

"How do *you* know him?" She forced her words to sound calm, rational.

"I met him when I was just starting out. He took me under his wing. I've known him now for years and he's become a good friend to my mother and Sabrina. A good man. Now he's retired and wasn't ready to completely retire so I hired him. We have a lot of retired cops."

She pushed away from Matt, trying desperately to separate what he'd just said from the person Matt was. He was speaking about him as though he were a saint. There was no way Matt would tolerate the kind of man Derek really was, but telling him that she hated Derek would mean having to share everything with him. So far, he'd been so understanding, hadn't pressured her at all. But now, if she said something specifically about Derek...

Matt was looking at her as though she was crazy. Maybe she was. "Why does it look like you think I'm suddenly an ass?"

She shook her head. Obviously, she wasn't doing a very good job of keeping things to herself. She grabbed her clothes from the ground and quickly dressed, knowing he could see her hands shaking, knowing that he had no idea what was going on. She couldn't stay here.

"He asked me about you."

A few minutes ago every inch of her had been bathed in heat, now she was frigid. He was back in her life, ruining it again. He had asked about her? She stood, trying to button her jeans, but her fingers were shaking so badly she couldn't. "How did he know about me?"

"I told him I was dating you."

Matt gently pulled her back down on the bed, but she didn't look at him. "Don't talk about me. Don't ever talk about me." Walls were closing in and her greatest nightmare was happening. He was here.

"Hey, Kate, you gotta talk to me, sweetheart. You can trust me."

She pushed out words that came from that dark place inside, that held all her memories and nightmares. She pushed the words past all her self-preservation instincts that told her not to speak. "What did he say about me?" Her voice sounded deep and hoarse. She stared down at her hands cupping her kneecaps as she braced herself for Matt's response. But whatever his response, she knew she needed to leave.

Matt let out a rough sigh. "It sounded like he knew you, like you had a past maybe."

She snapped her head to look at him. "What did he say? Exact words."

She read the surprise in Matt's eyes, caught the way his jaw clenched as he looked at her.

"Tell me what he said, Matt."

He stared into her eyes, and she knew he was studying her response. She braced herself. She knew he'd tell her the truth. "He told me to watch out. Something along the lines that you couldn't be trusted."

Rage swam through her in a torrential, fluid motion that rendered her speechless for a moment. Then she stood. "I need to go home."

He shrugged into his jeans and stood in front of her. He bent his knees slightly, trying to make eye contact with her. She knew she was playing into Derek's image of her. She knew she wasn't being fair to Matt. Maybe she was acting like a defiant child, or maybe she just didn't have what it took to be in a relationship. This would be the point in a normal, healthy relationship that she opened up, she would tell him, but she couldn't. How could she even begin to pull out each and every memory? Good or bad, they belonged deep inside, her own personal property.

Or what if she told Matt only the amount he needed to know? The part about Derek? The brief version? *Because he might not believe you, just like all of Derek's cop friends. How many times had she tried to tell Derek's cop friends what he was really like? They had all known. They had seen her mother's bruises, but not one of them had helped. They had all looked the other way. What if Matt believed Derek over her?* That would be too devastating.

"I want to go home, Matt," she whispered again.

"I defended you, I told him to back off. I told him you were a good person, and a mom."

"Whoa, you don't ever speak about me or Janie," she said, almost screaming, backing away from him.

"You need to tell me what the hell is going on."

"Does he live in Still Harbor?"

He shook his head. "No. The city. He commutes." He reached out, to cup her face she realized, but she had already flinched, already stepped back. He dropped his hands, his tanned face turning gray. He knew. He saw the fear. "You know you're safe here with me. You and Janie are safe."

She crossed her arms and nodded repeatedly, trying to distract herself from the sweet tenderness she heard in his deep voice, trying to resist the strong, warm man in front of her. If she truly trusted him she'd walk right to him, wrap her arms around him, and let him hear all of it.

"But you need to tell me why the thought of Derek living in Still Harbor terrifies you. I've known him forever. He's one of the good guys."

She squeezed her eyes shut, her heart breaking. "I need to go home."

"I know you, Kate. I know I'm not wrong. You don't want to talk. I won't make you talk. But stay here, with me."

Her secrets, the pain of what she was hiding, hung between them, thick and brutal. She bit her lower lip and looked up at the ceiling, blinking rapidly, watching the shadows from the fire flicker like the memories rolling through her head. But she didn't say a damn word.

"I have given you space, I haven't invaded your privacy even though I've been warned."

Her heart squeezed. "What the hell does that mean?"

"Well, generally when someone tells you to watch your back, you kind of want to know what that means."

"So, what? You'd do a background check on me?"

He clenched his jaw for a few beats, dropping his hands, before he gave a terse nod. "I didn't though because I assumed you'd eventually tell me."

"Well, eventually implies after time. It's barely been a few weeks. See, this is exactly why I didn't want to get involved. When you get involved with people they expect things from you that you don't want to share."

"So, what? You're just going to hide for the rest of your life?"

"I don't think I like you very much right now. You talked about me behind my back. You spoke about my *daughter*, you had no right. We are none of your business." Perhaps slightly juvenile, but true nonetheless. Despite how calm he was being, despite how appealing he looked in his fitted T-shirt and well-worn, low-slung jeans, the two-day scruff, and mussed up hair...this could go nowhere.

"You are my business now. You were in my bed. You know about my life, more than anyone else. Why did you come here?"

She frowned. "Because you invited me."

"You came here because you wanted me as much as I wanted you. You came here because you wanted to feel good, you couldn't ignore the attraction."

She held up her hand. "You need to know I've given you everything I can. I can't give more than this. I know your past, I know about Michelle."

"You're not my ex-wife, I'm not comparing you to her. And you haven't given me everything. You're talking like you're this person incapable of being honest."

"Honest? There's a difference between honesty and keeping things private."

He winced, looking impossibly confident, beautiful, unflappable. "Yeah. That's where this is going, that's where you know this is going, but for some reason you're denying it."

"Neither of us made promises. I can't deal with this. I didn't sign up for this. This whole interrogation about my life before you? I had a life and it was a shitty one for a long time. I will never be able to trust you the way you want me to." She knew perfectly well she wasn't being fair, she knew she was walking away from the only man she'd ever want. She couldn't give him the opportunity to decide whether he believed Derek or her. She'd rather be alone than see him side with a monster.

He cursed softly and ran his hands through his hair. His jaw was tense, his posture stiff. This was the first time she'd seen him thoroughly pissed. His eyes narrowed slightly as he looked into her eyes. "Did Derek hurt you?"

She squeezed her eyes shut and turned her back to him. Derek had hurt everything. The life she knew, the people she had clung to no longer existed because of him. "I need to get going. I don't regret any of...what we shared, but it went too far. If you still want to donate, it would be appreciated."

"You're kidding me. You are not walking out of here like we're business associates."

She started walking to the door. "You can't stop me. You won't stop me."

He grabbed her wrist, gently, but firmly. She stopped, looking down at the large hand on her skin, the hands she loved, that she welcomed, that she knew would protect her if she needed them to.

"That's an underlying threat, right? Or your little test to see if I'll manhandle you and make you stay here? I don't need to force you to stay. You can walk out of here, pretend like you're okay with leaving, but I know that you know it's bull. You want to be alone? Fine. I'll leave you alone. I was with a woman who didn't let me in. The only difference is that I didn't let her in either. I've let you in and now you're shutting me down. Fine, I made that mistake once before in my life, and ended up with a woman who cheated on me. I'd be a freaking idiot to do that twice."

The familiar sensation of being alone, of loss, crawled up Kate's body and wrapped around her neck, stealing any words that were capable of saving her.

He crossed the room with a few quick strides, opened a small box on his dresser, then turned to her. She braced herself for him to call her out on her cowardice, but he didn't. His mouth was pulled into a tight line, not the same mouth that had cherished every inch of skin on her body, and had spoken the most intoxicating words she'd ever heard in her life. His eyes still held the patience, the tenderness. "When you figure it out, act like the tough woman you pretend to be and come and find me. Let's go. I'll drive you home." He pressed a key into her hand and walked out the door.

Chapter Eleven

"Sara, sh, come here," Kate whispered, trying to be a big girl, dragging her little sister into the closet with her as the yelling grew louder. Usually Derek would duct tape her mouth shut so she couldn't scream, but she'd managed to sneak away before he remembered she and her sister were still in the apartment.

Derek screamed at their mother, "That is not my kid. Who were you screwing? You're a whore and that kid is going…"

Something crashed and Kate managed to shut the door, pulling Sara onto her lap, covering her little sister's ears until Derek stopped shouting.

"I have to help Mommy, you stay here, okay?" Sara nodded and Kate crept out of the closet silently reciting the prayer their mother said to them every night before bed, to give her strength, to block out Derek's mean words…Hail Mary, full of grace…she sucked in a breath as Derek threw an empty bottle of whiskey at her mother's head…the Lord is with thee… she screamed as her mother fell to the ground… Kate crouched over her, trying to breathe, nudging her mother to open her eyes…"Wake up, Mommy"… "Get the hell out of

*here, she's fine"...Derek slammed the door and left...Blessed
are thou amongst women...Kate rocked back and forth, the
words her only solace and began wringing her hands, over and
over until they bled...the prayer was supposed to help, it had
to help, that had to be why her mother said it every night...she
repeated the words, squeezing her eyes shut, waiting, waiting
until her mother woke, waiting until someone...until Matt
crouched beside her..."I've got you, Kate."*

Kate sat up in bed, clutching a pillow to her chest, gasping
for air. She swore and threw the pillow across the room. She
forced her breathing to slow, and she stumbled out of bed,
away from the dream.

Matt wasn't here. She could still feel him, the blanket
of safety that had been draped around her. She put on her
running shoes in the dark, fumbling with clumsy fingers as
she tied her shoelaces. She was already dressed for her run
because she knew the dreams would wake her up. A glance at
her alarm clock confirmed what she'd already expected: 4:48
a.m., the exact same time she had woken up all week.

Within minutes she was pounding the pavement with
her feet. She could run the route to the pier without thinking
about it. She rounded the last corner before the pier appeared
in the distance. Just as she had every other morning this week,
her gaze scanned the surroundings, looking for a glimpse of
a 6' 2", dark haired, gorgeous man and, as usual, he wasn't
there. No one was. Just her.

She forced her legs into a sprint. She'd round the
lighthouse and then go home. She'd get ready to face him
tomorrow night at the gala. Somehow, she was going to have
to face him without breaking down, without letting him in
again.

• • •

Matt knew, even as he rounded the lighthouse, that he wouldn't see Kate. He was half an hour later than her usual run time. He'd done that on purpose. He couldn't handle seeing her. After he'd driven her home, he knew that he needed distance from her. She had gotten to him, under his skin, and dammit she'd reached all the parts he'd shut off. He wanted her, all of her. He wanted her love.

His feet hit the pavement hard and he forced himself to keep going, despite the slow ache from his knee to his hip. The pain in his leg was nothing compared to what he felt when he thought about Kate.

He pulled his hood up as rain picked up from a drizzle to a downpour. All he saw was Kate, as she'd been the other night. Under him, on top of him, kissing him. The expression on her face, in her eyes as he'd entered her. And hell if he hadn't been completely floored to find out it was her first time. She'd been tight and so damn sweet. His bed still held her scent and he couldn't sleep because she wasn't there. He swore out loud as he stepped through a puddle, but it didn't even matter because he was already soaked by the rain.

He thought he'd held things close to his heart, but she took the prize. Derek. What the hell was going on? She'd walked away from him. She just chucked everything in favor of not confiding in him. It was that, that inability to open up to him, after everything they'd shared that made him lose it. He couldn't do that. He couldn't be with someone who wasn't 100 percent in.

So then, why wasn't he okay with how they left things?

Because he loved her. At the end of the day, despite whatever secrets she was holding on to, he loved her. He slowed his pace. He knew what he had to do. Maybe he was a moron, maybe he'd regret it, but he knew that even if he couldn't have her, he had to know she'd be okay, that she'd be safe.

He stopped by the row of benches and pulled out his cell phone, trying to slow his breath as he waited for Liam to pick up the phone.

"Holy hell, Matt. Why are you calling me so early?"

"Time to get your lazy ass out of bed," he said, forcing himself to sound somewhat calm. He looked out over the lake into the horizon, hating what he was about to do, but justifying it by his need to keep Kate and Janie safe.

"What do you want?"

"I need you to do some background checks."

"Okay, who?"

"Derek and Kate."

Liam swore. "Well, we did one automatically on Derek when he joined."

"No, I need more than that. I need you to dig deep and find out the connection between them. I need everything you can come up with. And, no one knows. Keep things normal with Derek. Tell me as soon as you find something."

"Done."

Matt wiped the rain off his face. "And, uh, Liam, I want you to put surveillance on Kate and her little girl, okay?"

He hung up the phone a second later, feeling the grim reality that someone very close to him was not who they appeared to be.

. . .

Matt leaned back in his chair and watched Kate as she gracefully made her way to the podium. The barn was packed, not that it looked like a barn anymore. The venue had been a surprising choice, but was perfect. The place was transformed with lights strung from the old beams and flowers and candles on all the tables, making it look like some high-end ballroom. What Kate, Alex, and Cara had accomplished was beyond admirable

His gaze swept over her, taking in the lush curves, beautifully highlighted in the floor-length navy dress. Her hair was up, with some pieces loose. He ached to pull it all down and feel it in his hands. He ached to have her alone and to himself. If everything went well, maybe by the end of the night that's exactly what would happen. It had killed him to let her walk away, to not stand there and fight for her, but he couldn't make her trust him or trust herself. As the week went on and there was no sign of her, he thought up another way that might accelerate the epiphany he was waiting for her to have.

He kept his gaze trained on her, waiting to see the exact moment she realized she would be introducing him tonight. He had called Cara and Alex the day before to tell them his news, swearing them to secrecy. Luckily, those two liked him and told him Kate was a wreck since she had left him. He was anxiously waiting for some information from Liam. His trust in Derek had vanished the night he'd asked Kate if he'd hurt her. The expression on her face hit him in the gut and kept him awake every night. He needed to make sure she was safe.

He was leaning back in his chair, ready to hear Kate introduce him to the packed room, when his phone vibrated in his suit pocket. He reached for it, making sure to still listen for his name. He glanced down at the screen. Sure enough, it was from Liam. *Go somewhere you can talk. This is big.*

Adrenaline pumped through his veins, along with dread, but he was trapped. Kate's sweet voice kept him connected to the night. "…my pleasure to introduce Matthew Lane."

He stood quietly, trying to push aside Liam's message. He would call him as soon as he finished his speech. It was fine, he told himself, as he wove through the tables, walking to the podium. Kate was here. He'd keep an eye on her and make sure she didn't leave alone. His muscles were tense, his blood pumping with the familiar rhythm of impending danger. Nothing was going to happen. He'd deal with whatever the hell was going on.

He joined her at the podium, his gaze locking on to hers. His heart lurched forward at the tortured look in her gorgeous eyes. There was no way they were over.

She stepped aside, and he cleared his throat, positioning himself behind the mike. He'd been brought up to never air his dirty laundry in public, to always put on a brave face. He'd watched the women he loved fall until they couldn't stand on their own anymore. He'd arrested bastards, men like his father. He'd crossed the line a few times, letting his own past influence his job. But tonight he was a guy who was just like any other adult who'd witnessed physical abuse growing up. And hell, if he had to lay it all out on the line for Kate, he was more than willing. If she needed more, in order to trust him, then he was ready.

He scanned the crowd before speaking. Kate, Alex, and Cara were near the front, eyes on him. Kate offered him a tiny smile and it took everything to turn away, to look at the crowd he was about to address. His gaze landed on something, someone, rather, that made him stand at attention. Derek was leaning against the bar, his eyes on Kate. The hair on the back of Matt's neck rose slowly and his instincts hummed in a way he couldn't ignore. There was something about the look in Derek's eye, the tilt of his head, the almost-sneer on his mouth. WTF? Derek wasn't supposed to be here.

He cleared his throat and glanced down at the written speech. He needed to get this done, and then get to Kate. "I'm honored to be here tonight. My name is Matthew Lane. I'm a former detective sergeant with the Ontario Provincial Police, I'm a partner in the Private Investigation Firm, JLI, and I'm proud to be donating the group home to the Still Harbor House for Women and Children." He paused as the crowd broke out into applause, but his gaze was on Kate. Her gorgeous mouth was open slightly, her chin wobbled, and the unmistakable sheen of tears glistened in her eyes. How the hell was he going to look away from that expression, from her? He needed to finish his speech. He glanced back at the crowd, ready to continue, when he noticed Derek wasn't standing near the bar anymore. He did a rapid scan of the room, but couldn't see him anywhere.

• • •

Kate willed her hand to stop trembling enough to at least insert the key into the lock. She'd driven here without even thinking twice about it. She felt safe here, in Matt's house. Seconds later, she heard the lock catch and she swung open the front door. Lights on sensors turned on and she locked the door behind her.

Rain splattered against the windows and she removed her heels before walking through to the kitchen. She stood there for a moment, taking deep breaths, watching as the rain made swirling patterns on the windows. Maybe she needed to pour herself a drink.

She slipped out of her heels and walked across the hardwood floor. She should have told Matt everything, not just the partial truth. She should have told him about Derek, but the idea that he wouldn't believe her, that he'd take his mentor and old friend's side over hers, had prevented her from telling him everything. How many times had she tried to repeat her story when she was small, when she actually believed that there were good people out there? The agony of having someone not believe her was unforgettable. With Matt she wouldn't be able to get over it. And then they'd be over, because she would never be able to have faith in him again.

But she couldn't be a coward forever.

She knew that tonight, the second she saw him. It had floored her. Yeah, so maybe it had taken her a long time to figure it out, but she had planned on coming here tonight to tell him the rest, to finally move forward. When he'd stood up there tonight, his strong body brushing against hers for the briefest of seconds before taking the mike, she had almost thrown her arms around him. The look in his eyes told her everything—she was done being afraid of him.

After his speech and his incredible donation, she'd attempted walking over to him, but a crowd surrounded him. She told Alex and Cara she was coming here to surprise him and snuck out the back. The reality was that she loved him and she needed to tell him everything.

The knock at the door jolted her out of her daydream. Without thinking twice about who it could be, she crossed the empty room and swung open the door. The man who starred in all her nightmares stood there. Derek.

She struggled for air and tried to shove the door shut, but he muscled his way in. She wasn't going to lose it. She had trained herself for this day, the day she would finally confront him as an adult, as an equal. She wasn't going down like she did when she was a little girl. There was no one here left to protect. There was no reason for her to keep her mouth shut. There was no duct tape for him to silence her with. This was Matt's place, her town, her life, and she'd be damned if he thought he had a right to this.

He barreled through the door and backed her into the closet door before she could even think. She knew she wasn't breathing; it was impossible to breathe. He pinned her against the door, his large hands clamped on her arms. "You're screwing up my life again. This ends now. Your relationship with Matt is over before I tell him the truth about what a lying little—"

"No," she said, taking a step closer to him. She didn't recognize her own voice. It was deep and hoarse, but there wasn't even a quiver in it. "You can tell him whatever you want, but then he'll listen to me, and I'll tell him what a wife-beating, murderer—"

He snatched her wrist and twisted it painfully. She practiced her breathing, focused, and kicked him hard in the groin, watching as he unhanded her and lost his footing. "What did you expect? That I was still afraid of you? I don't see any duct tape, so I guess you won't be able to shut me up." She was afraid of him still, the part of her deep down that was still the little girl that had witnessed his brutality, but she would never let on. Never.

"You actually think he's going to believe you? What, are you going to whisper in his ear and beg him to help you like you did with my partner that night? He won't believe you, he won't give a shit about something that happened over a decade ago. Get over it. He'll think you made a mistake, a stupid childhood mistake, and he'll believe me over your warped memories." She refused to remember the night he was talking about, her attempt to get help, her first attempt where an adult, a man sworn to protect, turned from her.

"You're a murdering bastard."

He glowered at her from his position on the floor. "You always blamed me for your mother and sister's death, but it wasn't my fault, I didn't kill them."

"You did, you forced her—"

"The truth is your mother didn't love you enough to stick around. If she had, she never would've jumped."

"You brutalized her, took advantage of a woman with mental illness, and never acknowledged Sara as your daughter. She was. She was your daughter and you never loved her because she wasn't perfect in your eyes. You're an asshole, Derek, and their deaths are on your dirty hands."

He shrugged, standing slowly, walking toward her. She held her ground. "What are you going to do, Kate? Maybe you can go stand in the corner and cry? Maybe you can wring your hands together until they bleed because you're such a little coward. You're so pathetic I won't even need to duct tape your mouth shut."

Acid churned choppily inside her stomach until she was almost certain she'd throw up. She tried to focus on his face, on this moment that she had fantasized about. She was able to confront this man now as an equal. She was an adult and she was finally able to call him out. "I'm not a little girl anymore, but you're still a murderer. Because of you, I don't have a mother or a sister."

He moved rapidly, pinning her against the wall, his hands on her throat. "I never wanted to hurt you. That wasn't my plan tonight. I wanted to come here and tell you to back off Matt."

"You wanted to shut me up," she hissed, silenced as his hands pressed on her windpipe painfully.

"I'm not leaving until you shut up and stay away from Matt. I want that job and I'm not going to have you ruining everything for me. When I finish telling him my version of what happened, he'll want nothing to do with you."

"What's your version? How you took advantage of a vulnerable woman? You berated her and blamed her for giving you a baby with Down's syndrome? You accused her of sleeping around? Sara was your baby. Your child, and you didn't deserve her. You didn't deserve either of them. You drove my mother to suicide."

"Shut up!"

"No, never. You will never shut me up again."

"What, you think because you're grown up you can take me on? You're just as pathetic as you were when you were a whiny little girl. You think that stupid kid you adopted is going to bring back your sister?"

She dug her nails into his skin as hard as she could, wanted to cause enough pain that he'd have to let her go, but instead he dug his hands harder, until her breath was caught and tears she refused to let fall filled her eyes.

He leaned down, breathing heavily, and she twisted her face away as he pressed his lips into her ear. "We're alone. There's no one here. There're lots of ways to shut you up, just like with your mom. What are you going to do now, Kate? You're so tough. What are you going to do? Beat me up?"

"No, I am."

Matt's deep, furious voice rang out. Suddenly, Derek's weight on her body, her soul, was lifted as Matt bulldozed him into the staircase. She shut her eyes and stifled the cry of freedom she wanted to shout out. How many times had she wanted someone to swoop in and rescue her? How many times had she prayed that someone would believe her? She had lost count, had stopped remembering. The number of times adults betrayed her had shattered her child self, and her adult self.

Matt knew nothing about what had happened. She hadn't let him in, she hadn't trusted him with her truths, but he was here now. He'd chosen her over Derek. He believed her without even asking for an explanation.

• • •

Matt heard his fist crack his friend's jaw, and he pulled back slightly. He held his mentor, his friend, pinned against the wall and tried to take a breath, tried to be rational, but he couldn't. He'd lost track of how many times he'd hit him. He'd lost track of where Kate was, he'd lost track of everything except the rage that kept his adrenaline high.

He'd pieced it all together, between the details from

Liam regarding Kate's mother's and sister's deaths and Kate's reaction to Derek. He didn't need to know the rest of the details to know that he'd been an idiot to ever trust this man.

"Matt, son…"

"I'm not your son, you are nothing to me."

"She's lying," Derek said, pausing to spit blood out of his mouth. "She's a lying, filthy whore and—"

He cut off Derek's words by slamming his head against the wall.

"Shit, Matt. Good enough, we don't want him to have to go to the hospital." He tore his eyes from Derek's face to look at Liam. He didn't even know when his friend had gotten here.

"Let go, I'll take it from here," Liam said, prying his hands off Derek. Derek slumped to the ground. Liam's face was grim as he pulled Derek back up to his feet.

"What do you want me to do with him?"

Matt tried to catch his breath, tried to focus. "Take him to his apartment. Let him pack a bag, clean himself up and then put him on a bus out of the province."

"Derek," Matt yelled, shaking him until he opened his eyes. "You get the hell out of the province, you come anywhere near us and you're a dead man." Derek winced and shut his eyes. "Understand?" Matt yelled.

Derek slowly nodded.

Liam clasped Matt's shoulder. "You okay?"

Matt nodded, trying to let some of his rage drain out of him. Liam looked over his shoulder and he nodded at Kate before leaving the house.

Matt forced himself to calm down, to let go of some of his rage before he turned around to face Kate. He clenched his hands, stuffed them in his pockets, and slowly turned around.

She was standing in the hallway, still, white, and looking so unlike the tough girl he'd nicknamed her. She looked small and afraid and it made him angry all over again. Tears streamed down her cheeks and her hair was a mess, tangled from where that bastard had touched her. He stood there, and it was one of the very few moments in his life where he didn't know what the hell he should do. He wanted to walk up to her and hold her forever. But he didn't know how she'd react. Right now, she looked scared and small and it made him so damn pissed to see that.

"Matt," she whispered and then she was running to him. He held her hard against him, willing her to feel safe, loved.

"I came here to tell you I was sorry," she whispered against his chest. "To thank you."

"I'm sorry I wasn't here," he said against her hair.

Her hands dug into his sides and he knew she was struggling for control.

"Come on," he said, slowly pulling her into the family room. He sat her on the couch. He pulled the blanket from the back of the couch, feeling how cold she was. "I'm going to light the fire and get us a drink," he said, walking around the room. She didn't say a word. Minutes later he was back in the room, the fireplace on.

"Here, sweetheart," Matt said, handing Kate a glass of whiskey. He sat down, wrapping her up in his arms, not ever wanting to let her go.

Tonight had been filled with revelations. He knew in his gut that he loved Kate, but it wasn't until he walked into his home to find Derek with his hands on her that he knew the extent of his love for her. At that moment, all that mattered was Kate, and he'd been willing to do anything.

She leaned back against him with a sigh. "Your limp is back," she whispered. He kissed her neck, taking a sip from the glass they shared.

"I'm okay," he said roughly. "I'm also feeling like an asshole for not knowing about Derek. I almost got here too late."

"How could you know? I didn't tell you a thing."

"I ran that background check on Derek, and yeah, nothing came up. But Liam did some digging, called in some trusted contacts and started piecing together quite the story. That's why I walked out tonight. Liam called and I needed to hear it. Then when I came back in, you were gone and so was Derek."

She looked down and held out her hand for the glass, finishing off the contents. "I didn't know he was there," she whispered.

"Why did you come here?"

"I wanted to be with you. I was coming here to tell you how much I missed you and I wanted to tell you everything," she said in a small voice that tore at him.

He kissed the top of her head and waited.

"It's not something I talk about, with anyone, but I should have been honest with you, I should have trusted you. I, uh, I was shut down a lot as a child when I would try and explain what was happening at home. And even though I know it's irrational and that I'm an adult now, a part of me thinks no one will believe me." She turned in his arms, to look at him, her knees tucked up to her chest. Her green eyes met his gaze, punched him in the gut with something that looked a helluva lot like love shining in them. "You believed me without knowing a thing."

He leaned down to kiss her, slowly, gently, and then pulled back before they both got distracted. He wanted to know all of it, all the missing pieces about her. He moved her hair back, kissed her neck and whispered, "I'll always believe you."

She leaned back into him, and he knew the trust she must have in him now. "My mother and father had a good marriage. Not a lot of money, but they were young and in love and none of that seemed to matter, until he died of a massive heart attack. I was only six and, honestly, I barely remember him, but I do have a distinct memory of being *happy*. My mom struggled for a year...and then she met Derek, this big, burly cop who promised her everything. I don't blame her for choosing him. He got her when she was at a low point. They got married and everything was fine, he was even decent to me. And then a few months later the real Derek started coming home. What's that expression, about a wolf in sheep's clothing? Yeah. Little things would set him off like dinner not being ready on time, if I left my toys out in the family room, if there wasn't any beer in the fridge. I hated him so much, Matt."

He put his chin on her shoulder, hugging her tighter, wanting to reach out to that little girl who had lost her mother. He knew the kind of abuse she was talking about. This part of their childhoods was, sadly, very similar.

"Then she got pregnant. He was happy, but it still didn't stop him from knocking her around. I remember pleading with her to leave. I told her I could drop out of school and get a job. What job an eight-year-old could get is beyond me," she said with a little laugh. "But no, she was trapped. She wouldn't leave. And then my little sister, Sara, was born. She was perfect, but she had Down's syndrome. Derek was so angry. He said the most awful things to my mother. He accused her of sleeping around, claiming he never could have fathered a child like Sara. He wore her down. Pretty soon, I barely recognized my mother anymore. There were some days I'd get a glimmer of the mom she was before. We'd go for walks with Sara or read stories...and then when I was fifteen..." She took a long, shaky breath and put her head on her knees.

"She killed herself, Matt, and she took Sara with her. She told me that morning that I was invincible, and then she was gone."

Matt shut his eyes. He had seen a lot of shit. Shit that still turned his stomach. He knew all about the disgusting people in the world, the truly evil scum that made you not care whether they lived or died. If they died you'd have the safety of knowing they were gone, and if they lived, but were behind bars, you'd have the satisfaction of knowing the rest of their life was going to be crap. But as a cop, as a person hearing a news story, you were a few degrees removed and you could drink yourself under the table until you were numb. But knowing the person you loved had lived through this kind of thing...there was no alcohol that took away the ache.

"I think she took Sara because she knew...she was afraid of what would happen to her." Her words were muffled and he smoothed her hair, trying to come up with anything that would sound remotely helpful, but he knew nothing could help.

"What happened to you?"

She shrugged. "I ran away. I stole three hundred dollars from the envelope I knew Derek kept under his mattress. I stuffed my backpack with the essentials and I was gone. I couldn't live with him. As far as I was concerned, he was a murderer. I don't care that they called it suicide. He murdered her. Slowly. Every day. From the inside out, he killed her."

Matt blinked against the moisture in his eyes. *Hell.*

"I hid at some friends' houses, the friends whose parents were never around. Then I just took off one day. After a while I walked into a shelter and I met Cara and Alex, both as scared and quiet as me. I'll never forget that long table in the dining room of that old house. The three of us made eye contact and something happened. I couldn't explain it, why I felt this insane connection to them, but it was there, in their eyes. It was like I had found family. I never thought I'd have a family again, until that day.

We became best friends. We all stayed there together for a few years, but then we were separated. We made a pact to stay in touch, to live together one day, and to adopt some kids in need. I saw school as my quick ticket to a good paying job. All I did in those group homes was study. I finished high school a year early, got a full scholarship, and did my undergrad early as well. I was so focused on getting to the end game, I couldn't have cared less about the whole university experience."

"I wish I'd known you then."

"You wouldn't have stood a chance."

He laughed softly as he kissed her neck. "I have my ways. I can be very persuasive, especially when I want something badly. And you, you I want very badly. Not just in bed, or for a day here and there, but for forever. You. Janie. A family. I want it with you. I swore I'd never do it again, but with you I will. I'd do anything for you. I love you."

Kate stared at him, then placed her hand on his strong jaw, needing to feel him, to make certain he was real. "When I was little I'd dream about a family of my own, and then I just sort of gave up on that, on believing in the good guy. I thought they didn't exist, but they do. You do. You're the good guy. The best. I love you, Matt."

"You'll always have a home with me. You'll always be safe with me. We'll figure out what we're going to do about Derek."

"I don't want to deal with him. I don't want to think about him."

Matt didn't say anything. She'd been through enough tonight, but he knew they'd have to look at options. At the end of the day, he wanted her to feel safe, whatever the cost.

"You know when I got mad at you for defending Janie at the restaurant?"

"Yeah?"

"I was envious of you. I love that you don't care what people think, that you don't stop and worry. You act. When people you care about are hurt, you act. I think it just made me so aware that I have failed in that department. Sometimes it would feel like Derek had duct tape on my mouth, that it was safer to stay quiet."

His arms constricted, keeping her close. "I learned how to defend people at a young age. We had different ways. Don't ever beat yourself up. You've got guts, Kate, you're stubborn as hell, and you're going to conquer the last of your fears. You can practice yelling at me," he said, smiling at the sound of her laughter.

"We can practice lots of things," she said, turning now to look at him. And then she did that thing when she framed his face with her soft hands. She looked tired, spent, but she looked loved. She looked beautiful.

He leaned forward and captured her mouth in a kiss that took them both far away from the kids they once were, from the pain they had lived through. He kissed her with the promise of forever. He tasted the woman he'd wanted from the moment he'd laid eyes on her and she tasted so damn sweet, so damn perfect that he held on tighter. She was the woman made for him, and he loved her in a way that was all-consuming. She and Janie brought out the good in him. She believed in him.

Kate completed every missing piece of him; she made him a better man. Kate was in his blood, she was his soul.

Epilogue

Matt stood on the porch, his hand on the doorknob. He couldn't go in just yet. He stood and watched his family inside the empty house. He gripped the edges of the paper take-out bags in his hands and tried to forget the meeting he'd just come from.

But he couldn't, because all those women inside the house were his family. Hell, he'd had a hard enough time with just his mother and sister, but now...it was all of them. Kate, her sisters, the kids. He'd do anything for them. For Kate, for Janie. They had given him everything. Kate had given him all of her, and he knew no woman would ever be able to touch him the way she had.

He had thought the bullshit was all gone, all the threats to their happiness gone, but he had gotten some crazy-ass news about Alex and her little girl. Shit, it would send her and her daughter's life in an entirely new direction if it was true.

How the hell was he going to tell them?

The door swung open, the woman on the other side of it evoking a rush of love and desire every single time he saw her.

"It's about time you got here, detective."

He grinned at her and then hauled her out onto the porch for a moment of privacy. She wrapped her arms around his neck and kissed him.

"What's the earliest acceptable time to leave?" he whispered against her lips.

"We're out of luck tonight. We'll be here late. What's that delicious smell?"

He reluctantly pulled himself away and picked up the bag of abandoned takeout. "Let's go inside." The news he had wasn't forgotten, but as he walked into the house and looked at the women, he knew he couldn't do this tonight. Tomorrow.

• • •

"I got poutine for all of us."

Matt's statement was met with a round of complaints and groans. Kate laughed and slapped a kiss on his mouth that lasted a tad longer than it should have, considering the audience.

They—Alex, Cara, the girls, and Matt's mother and sister—were all hard at work in the new Still Harbor House for Women and Children. She knew this wouldn't have happened, this fast, this early, without Matt. It was only mid-November and they had taken possession of the house. Despite the fact that it needed a lot of work, it was a major step.

"Sorry I'm late," Matt said, handing her the bags of food as he slipped out of his jacket. Her gaze roamed over him appreciatively, still not used to him, to her attraction to him. Everything was better every day; everything was better with him.

"Everything okay?" Now that they were inside, she could see the telltale worry lines in his forehead. She knew there were certain aspects of his job that still bothered him, but she could feel the tension in him.

"Maaaatttt!" They were interrupted as Janie ran over to him. He leaned down and scooped her up. Janie snuggled into his chest and he looked over at Kate, smiling. This was the guy she'd met at the bar, the guy who'd continued to stand up for them. She'd leaned on him enough that most of her memories were fading, replaced by the good feelings he evoked.

"All right, we're starving. Let's eat this awful food you seem to be obsessed with," Sabrina said, rifling through the bags. "Seriously, it's not fair that you can eat like this and not gain any weight."

"You're the one who told me about this place. Jog with us."

"I'd rather die."

"Drama."

"Now that's enough. There are dear children in the room," Barb said, admonishing them both. They laid out a picnic blanket and sat down and ate together. Kate looked around at all of them, at Alex and Cara, their gazes locking. How much had changed since they had first met? They were older. They had all survived their own hell, and were now here, safe and living their dreams. She hoped for them that they'd each find a man as good as Matt to make them as happy as she was.

She looked over at their girls, giggling and spilling food all over the blanket, at the unicorn that was looming over the picnic blanket, at the guy who had won her daughter the unicorn, and had won her heart. Matt was watching her in a way that made her feel cherished, loved. When his eyes dipped lower, stopping on her lips, then traveling down the rest of her body, she felt the passion that grew with every passing day.

He grabbed her hand gently, tugging her toward the door. "Come here, I have something to show you."

"I've seen it before, not appropriate."

He laughed as he gave her a kiss. "Not that, smart-ass. Outside. Come on."

She followed him around the side of the house, stepping around construction planks and debris. He unlocked the back gate and held it open for her. He was grinning at her and she couldn't help but smile. "You're not usually this mysterious."

"I'm a man with many layers," he said. "Close your eyes and take my hand." He held out his hand and waited.

She smiled at him, at the mischievous, boyish expression on his face, and then placed her hand in his. "I trust you, even though this backyard is a minefield with all the mess from the landscaping company."

He gave her a quick kiss and slowly led her further into the large yard. "Okay, stop," he said a few minutes later. "You can open your eyes now."

She blinked a few times to focus, to grasp the significance. They were enveloped in the dark cocoon of night, the only light coming from the fountain in front of them. There was a rock wall, and a steady stream of water poured down like a waterfall into a circular pool. The waterfall was backlit and Matt gently pulled her closer until she noticed the plaque. She read the inscription aloud: "In loving memory of Darlene and Sara Abbott."

Emotion flooded through her and she spun around to look at Matt. "Thank you," she whispered, throwing herself into his arms. Just like always, he wrapped his arms around her and held her close.

"You're welcome. I thought it would be a good way to remember them. Maybe it will bring some of the women and kids in this house some peace too, as they try and rebuild their lives."

She blinked back tears as she stared into his eyes. She had memories of her mother and Sara that were forever engraved on her heart, on her soul. She carried them with her wherever she went, and they carried her on her darkest days, forcing her to move forward. But this man, Matt, had managed to capture the parts of her that she thought didn't exist anymore. He'd healed her.

He'd saved her, he'd loved her, and he'd never stopped believing in her. He was the guy she never even dared to dream up, because he was too perfect, because she thought guys like him couldn't exist. But he did. He was here and he was hers. Matt, Janie, and her sisters were her family. The family she had once known, the little girl she once was, no longer existed. But what they all were was so much stronger, more beautiful than she could have believed.

He leaned down, capturing her mouth in a kiss. He would always be there for her; he would always come through for her. He'd taken away her fears, shown her love, passion. He'd believed her.

He pulled back slightly, brushing his lips against hers. "I love you so much, Kate."

"I love you too, Mr. Zibbits."

He laughed against her mouth before kissing her again.

About the Author

Victoria James always knew she wanted to be a writer and in grade five, she penned her first story, bound it (with staples) and a cardboard cover and did all the illustrations herself. Luckily, this book will never see the light of day again.

In high school she fell in love with historical romance and then contemporary romance. After graduating University with an English Literature degree, Victoria pursued a degree in interior design and then opened her own business. After her first child, Victoria knew it was time to fulfill the dream of writing romantic fiction.

Victoria is a hopeless romantic who is living her dream, penning happily-ever-after's for her characters in between managing kids and the family business. Writing on a laptop in the middle of the country in a rambling old Victorian house would be ideal, but she's quite content living in suburbia with her husband, their two young children, and very bad cat.

Visit her website: www.victoriajames.ca

Don't miss the next book in the **Still Harbor** *series...*

FALLING FOR HER ENEMY

Find your Bliss with these great releases...

BETTING ON LOVE
a His Reason to Stay novel by Jennifer Hoopes

All Sam Ellis does is work. Concerned, his siblings bet he can't keep a girlfriend for thirty days. If he loses, he's out as CEO. No problem, he can fake a relationship. Whitney Carroll is back home in Gatlinburg, Tennessee after divorcing her low-down, cheating husband. Sam hires Whitney for a job and as his fake girlfriend. Their connection is undeniable but when disaster strikes, are they willing to trade their jobs for their hearts?

THE KISS LIST
a Love List novel by Sonya Weiss

All Haley has ever wanted was her One True Love. Her parents knew they were soul mates at their first kiss, so surely Haley will, too, if she can just kiss each guy on her foolproof Kiss List. Enter Max: bane of Haley's existence but unfortunately, as a local, her way in with the guys. Max wants nothing to do with love or Haley, but the more time they spend together, the clearer it is that there's a paper-thin line between love and hate...

Claiming the Doctor's Heart
a novel by Sean D. Young

When his father is hospitalized, Dr. Eric Bradley must fill in for him as the small-town doctor. Without Holly Ransom, the receptionist, to keep things running smoothly, he wouldn't survive. If only her sweet n' sassy charm were enough to solve all his problems. Eric must leave in a month or he'll lose the opportunity of a lifetime. But how can he leave the woman he's falling in love with and his family legacy behind?

Just One Kiss
an Appletree Cove novel by Traci Hall

Free-spirited Grace Sheldon owes thirty thousand dollars on the house she's inherited. Her freelance photography definitely won't cover that. So, she opts for a temp job…at a dog training facility. Sawyer Rivera relishes his quiet life. Until his new office assistant, who knows more about chickens than the dogs he trains, comes crashing through his door. The woman is his complete opposite—and yet completely refreshing. Now Sawyer has one chance to try to change their fate before Grace's month of temp work is over.